PAST PERFECT, PRESENT TENSE

Also by Richard Peck

Novels for Young Adults
Amanda/Miranda
Are You in the House Alone?
Bel-Air Bambi and the Mall Rats
Blossom Culp and the Sleep of Death
Close Enough to Touch
Don't Look and It Won't Hurt
The Dreadful Future of Blossom Culp
Dreamland Lake
Fair Weather
Father Figure
The Ghost Belonged to Me
Ghosts I Have Been
The Great Interactive Dream Machine
The Last Safe Place on Earth
A Long Way from Chicago
Lost in Cyberspace
Princess Ashley
Remembering the Good Times
Representing Super Doll
The River Between Us
Secrets of the Shopping Mall
Strays Like Us
Those Summer Girls I Never Met
Through a Brief Darkness
Unfinished Portrait of Jessica
Voices After Midnight
A Year Down Yonder

Novels for Adults
Amanda/Miranda
London Holiday
New York Time
This Family of Women

Picture Book
Monster Night at Grandma's House

Nonfiction
Anonymously Yours
Invitations to the World

PAST PERFECT, PRESENT TENSE

New and Collected Stories

by

Richard Peck

Dial Books  New York

Published by Dial Books
A member of Penguin Group (USA) Inc.
345 Hudson Street, New York, New York 10014
Copyright © 2004 by Richard Peck

"Priscilla and the Wimps" previously appeared in *Sixteen,* edited by Donald R. Gallo, Delacorte Press, 1984.
"The Electric Summer" first appeared in *Time Capsule,* edited by Donald R. Gallo, Delacorte Press, 1999.
"Shotgun Cheatham's Last Night Above Ground" first appeared in *Twelve Shots,* edited by Harry Mazer, Delacorte Books for Young Readers, 1997.
"The Special Powers of Blossom Culp" first appeared in *Birthday Surprises,* edited by Johanna Hurwitz, Morrow Junior Books/HarperCollins Children's Books, 1995.
"Girl at the Window" first appeared in *Night Terrors,* edited by Lois Duncan, Aladdin Paperbacks, Simon & Schuster, 1996.
"The Most Important Night of Melanie's Life" first appeared in *From One Experience to Another,* edited by M. Jerry Weiss and Helen S. Weiss, Forge Books, Tom Doherty Associates, 1997.
"Waiting for Sebastian" first appeared in *Dirty Laundry,* edited by Lisa Rowe Fraustino, Viking Books, 1988.
"Shadows" first appeared in *Visions,* edited by Donald R. Gallo, Delacorte Press, 1987.
"I Go Along" first appeared in *Connections,* edited by Donald R. Gallo, Delacorte Press, 1989.
"The Kiss in the Carry-on Bag" first appeared in *Destination Unexpected,* edited by Donald R. Gallo, Candlewick Press, 2003.
"The Three-Century Woman" first appeared in *Second Sight,* Philomel Books, 1999.

Designed by Lily Malcom
Text set in Granjon
Printed in the U.S.A. on acid-free paper
10 9 8 7 6 5 4 3 2 1

Library of Congress Cataloging-in-Publication Data
Peck, Richard.
    Past perfect, present tense : new and collected stories / Richard Peck.
        p. cm.
Summary: A collection of short stories, including two previously
unpublished ones, that deal with the way things could be.
    ISBN 0-8037-2998-7
    1. Children's stories, American. [1. Short stories.] I. Title.
PZ7.P338Wh 2004   [Fic]—dc22
2003010904

To Marcia and John Servente

Acknowledgments

I acknowledge with thanks the editors who
generously have included my work in their
anthologies:

Lois Duncan
Lisa Rowe Fraustino
Donald R. Gallo
Michael Green
Johanna Hurwitz
Harry Mazer
M. Jerry Weiss and
Helen Weiss

I am grateful to Roger Sutton, who encouraged
this collection.

CONTENTS

INTRODUCTION 1

THE FIRST 7

Priscilla and the Wimps 9

THE PAST 15

The Electric Summer 21
Shotgun Cheatham's Last Night Above Ground 36
The Special Powers of Blossom Culp 50
By Far the Worst Pupil at Long Point School 60

THE SUPERNATURAL 67

Girl at the Window 71
The Most Important Night of Melanie's Life 82
Waiting for Sebastian 90
Shadows 100

THE PRESENT 111

Fluffy the Gangbuster 115
I Go Along 132
The Kiss in the Carry-on Bag 141
The Three-Century Woman 157

HOW TO WRITE A SHORT STORY 167

FIVE HELPFUL HINTS 171

# Introduction

A short story, like fiction of any length, is always about change. Even in a handful of pages, the characters can't be the same people in the last paragraph whom we met in the first. If there's no change, there's no story, unless you write fiction for *The New Yorker* magazine.

A word writers use is "epiphany." In ancient Greece the word described the miraculous appearance of a god or goddess. The Christian church uses the word with a capital *E* to define Twelfth Night, the moment when the Magi, the Three

Kings, made the long-heralded discovery of the Christ child.

In fiction writing, the epiphany is a sudden breakthrough of understanding, of self-awareness. It's that moment of change that changes every moment after. It's the lightbulb switched suddenly on over somebody's head. Novels tell of epiphanies acted upon. A short story tends to turn upon a single epiphany, sometimes in the last line. The change to come is to play out in the reader's mind.

In real life we have epiphanies all the time. But we wait for them to go away. Change is too hard, and threatening. That's why we have fiction. Stories are better than real life, or we wouldn't have them. Stories for the young present the metaphor of change upon the page to prepare the readers for the changes coming in their lives. Non-readers will never be ready.

Again, like all fiction, a short story is never an answer, always a question. Writers with answers write nonfiction: advice columns and government pamphlets and textbooks. Fiction writers have only questions, and the eternal question all fiction asks the reader is:

WHAT IF I WERE THE CHARACTER IN THIS STORY?
WHAT WOULD *I* DO?

This is the great gift readers receive: They can be anybody and go anywhere. They can try on all these lives to see which ones fit.

Stories raise every kind of question. Stories for the young regularly invite their readers to ask themselves:

WHEN WILL I START TAKING CHARGE OF MY LIFE?

A comic story can ask serious questions. So can a tale of the supernatural, which is only another device for questioning actual people and wondering how they work. A story set in past times can ask a modern reader timeless questions about all those issues history and progress never solve. Even an animal character can be a way of asking what moves and motivates humans. Fiction writers creep up on as many sides of their readers as they can. They use as many techniques as they can think of.

And so a short story is like all fiction: It's a question about change.

All stories begin with those same two words:

WHAT IF?

A story isn't what is. It's what if? Fiction isn't real life with the names changed. It's an alternate reality to reflect the reader's own world.

But what is a short story not? It's not a condensation of a novel, or an unfinished one. It's not Cliffs Notes to anything. It has its own shape and profile. It's not the New York skyline; it's a single church spire. Its end is much nearer its beginning, and so it can be overlooked.

"One tends to overpraise a long book because one has got through it," said E. M. Forster—a novelist. His tongue was in his cheek, but he makes a point. A full-length novel with its community of characters, its multiple epiphanies, its changing scenes, is taken more seriously—in class, in reviews, in the book club.

The short story is much misunderstood. There are even aspiring writers who think they'll start out writing short stories and work their way up to the big time: novels. It doesn't work like that. A short story isn't easier than a novel. It has so little space to make its mark that it requires the kind of self-mutilating editing most new writers aren't capable of. It has less time to plead its case.

Only poetry is less forgiving. But poetry can teach you how to throw out all the words that aren't pulling their weight. In a short story there's no place to hide, whether you're the writer or the reader.

I hadn't meant to be a short-story writer. I'd hoped to be Mark Twain. The first of his books to lift me out of my world and into a bigger one was *Life on the Mississippi*.

It seemed to be autobiography, and true. I little knew how much fictional technique, and fiction, that book embodied. I fell for nonfiction, the romance of the real.

But later when I was a teacher, an English teacher naturally, my students preferred fiction to reality. They were in junior high, and so they preferred ANYTHING to reality. But our curriculum was heavy-laden with full-length novels, even when I drew up the reading list myself. I harbored the wan hope of stretching their attention spans.

Junior-high teaching made a writer out of me. The first question a writer has to answer before putting pen to paper is:

WHO ARE THE PEOPLE WHO MIGHT BE WILLING TO READ WHAT I MIGHT BE ABLE TO WRITE?

I found those people in my roll book. They were the people I knew the best, and liked the best. From our first morning together I knew things about them their parents dared never know. Better yet, as their English teacher I saw in their compositions what they would never say aloud within the hearing of their powerful peers. The voices in their pages still ring in mine.

When I quit teaching to write, I had novels in mind. First one, to see if I could do it, and now thirty-two novels through these thirty-two years later. But as the years went by, the short story found its own way into my career.

Most of the short stories in this collection were written as assignments. Editors like Donald R. Gallo and Michael Green, writing colleagues like Lois Duncan and Harry Mazer, ask us to write short stories for collections they're putting together. Sometimes they give us a theme, sometimes not. Sometimes they give us the length, sometimes not. They always give us deadlines. Real life turns out to be strangely like school: You have assignments—and deadlines. Yet deadlines are our friends. The deadline helps us find the time to write the story.

But how much easier to talk about writing than to write. How much easier to generalize about a whole generation of readers than to reach just one of them upon the shared page . . .

The First

The first short story stands alone because it's the first one I ever wrote. And because it may be the most widely read of anything I've ever written, of any length. From this story, I learned that short stories can go places novels can't—into textbook anthologies and other people's collections and endless magazine reprints in any number of languages.

This one goes first because it proves that a writer can't have a master plan for his career. A writer has to be ready to turn on a dime.

One day more than twenty-five years ago, I was bent over the typewriter in the midst of a novel when the phone rang. It was the editor of a magazine for teenagers. She said she'd been reading my novels and wanted me to write a short story for her magazine. It had to be set in junior high/middle school. She already had too many stories about high school.

When I could get a word in, I told her I didn't do short stories.

"We pay three hundred dollars," she said.

"I'll try," I said.

"It has to be very short," she said, "about a thousand words, and it needs to end with a bang. That's the good news. The bad news is that we'll need it by Thursday."

She hung up, and I had thirty-six hours to write my first short story. All I knew about it was that it had to be set in junior high, so I assumed the girl would be bigger than the boy. The story unfolded from there.

I knew too that I wouldn't be working on my novel for thirty-six hours, that I wouldn't be leaving the house, that I'd be bringing my meals to the desk.

What I didn't know was that years later in another century, I'd be putting together a collection of my short stories because of that one and how it opened a new door.

I called it "Priscilla and the Wimps."

Priscilla and the Wimps

Listen, there was a time when you couldn't even go to the *restroom* around this school without a pass. And I'm not talking about those little pink tickets made out by some teacher. I'm talking about a pass that would cost anywhere up to a buck, sold by Monk Klutter.

Not that Mighty Monk ever touched money, not in public. The gang he ran, which ran the school for him, was his collection agency. They were Klutter's Kobras, a name spelled out in nailheads on six well-know black plastic windbreakers.

Monk's threads were more . . . subtle. A pile-lined suede battle jacket with lizard-skin flaps over tailored Levi's and a pair of ostrich-skin boots, brass-toed and suitable for kicking people around. One of his Kobras did nothing all day but walk a half step behind Monk, carrying a fitted bag with Monk's gym shoes, a coil of restroom passes, a cash box, and a switch-blade that Monk gave himself manicures with at lunch over at the Kobras' table.

Speaking of lunch, there were cases of advanced malnutri-tion among the newer kids. The ones who were a little slow in handing over a cut of their lunch money and were therefore barred from the cafeteria. Monk ran a tight ship.

I admit it. I'm five foot five, but when the Kobras slithered by, with or without Monk, I shrank. And I admit this too: I paid up on a regular basis. And I might add: so would you.

This school was old Monk's Garden of Eden. Unfortu-nately for him, there was a serpent in it. The reason Monk didn't recognize trouble when it was staring him in the face is that the serpent in the Kobras' Eden was a girl.

Practically every guy in school could show you his scars. Fang marks from Kobras, you might say: lumps, lacerations, blue bruises. But girls usually got off with a warning.

Except there was this one girl named Priscilla Roseberry. Picture a girl named Priscilla Roseberry, and you'll be light years off. Priscilla was, hands down, the largest student in the school. I'm not talking fat. I'm talking big. Even beautiful, in a bionic way. Priscilla wasn't inclined toward organized crime.

Otherwise, she could have put together a gang that would turn Klutter's Kobras into a bunch of garter snakes.

Priscilla was basically a loner except she had one friend, a little guy named Melvin Detweiler. You talk about The Odd Couple. Melvin's one of the smallest guys above midget status ever seen. They even had lockers next to each other in the same bank as mine. I don't know what they had going. I'm not saying this was a romance. After all, people deserve their privacy.

Priscilla was sort of above everything, if you'll pardon a pun. And very calm, as only the very big can be. If there was anybody who didn't notice Klutter's Kobras, it was Priscilla.

Until one winter day after school when we were all grabbing our coats out of our lockers. And hurrying, since Klutter's Kobras made sweeps of the halls for after-school shakedowns.

Anyway, up to Melvin's locker swaggers one of the Kobras. Never mind his name. Gang members don't need names. They have group identity. He reaches down and grabs little Melvin by the neck and slams his head against his locker door. The sound of skull against steel rippled all the way down the locker now, speeding the crowds on their way.

"Okay, let's see your pass," snarls the Kobra.

"A pass for what this time?" Melvin asks, probably still dazed.

"Let's call it a pass for very short people," says the Kobra. "A dwarf tax." He wheezes a little Kobra chuckle, and already he's reaching for Melvin's wallet with the hand that isn't circling Melvin's windpipe. All this time, of course, Melvin and the Kobra are standing in Priscilla's big shadow.

She's taking her time shoving her books into her locker and pulling on an extra-large coat. Then, quicker than the eye, she brings the side of her enormous hand down in a chop that breaks the Kobra's hold on Melvin's throat. You could hear a pin drop in that hallway. Nobody'd ever laid a finger on a Kobra, let alone a hand the size of Priscilla's.

Then Priscilla, who hardly every says anything to anybody except to Melvin, says to the Kobra, "Who's your leader, wimp?"

This practically blows the Kobra away. First he's chopped by a girl. Now she's acting like she doesn't know Monk Klutter, the Head Honcho of the World. He's so amazed, he tells her. "Monk Klutter."

"Never heard of him," Priscilla mentions. "Send him to see me." The Kobra just backs away from her like the whole situation is too big for him, which it is.

Pretty soon Monk himself slides up. He jerks his head once, and his Kobras slither off down the hall. He's going to handle this interesting case personally. "Who is it around here doesn't know Monk Klutter?"

He's standing inches from Priscilla, but since he'd have to look up at her, he doesn't. "Never heard of him," says Priscilla.

Monk's not happy with this answer, but now he's spotted Melvin, who's growing smaller in spite of himself. Monk breaks his own rule by reaching for Melvin with his own hands. "Kid," he says, "you're going to have to educate your girlfriend."

His hands never quite make it to Melvin. In a move of pure poetry Priscilla has Monk in a hammerlock. His neck's popping like gunfire, and his head's bowed under the immense weight of her forearm. His suede jacket's peeling back, showing pile.

Priscilla's behind him in another easy motion. With a single mighty thrust forward, she frog-marches Monk into her own locker. It's incredible. His ostrich-skin boots click once in the air. And suddenly he's gone, neatly wedged into the locker, a perfect fit. Priscilla bangs the door shut, twirls the lock, and strolls out of school. Melvin goes with her, of course, trotting along below her shoulder. The last stragglers leave quietly.

Well, this is where fate, an even bigger force than Priscilla steps in. It snows all that night, a blizzard. The whole town ices up. School closes for a week.

The Past

I call 1900 the year of my birth,
but Mama claims to have no idea of the day.
—"The Special Powers of Blossom Culp"

These next four stories appear together because they're set in the past, and the past is my favorite place. All fiction is historical fiction the minute the ink is dry, particularly if you write for the young.

Very little history is learned in school or college now, but that only spurs on the fiction writer. Whole generations of us fell for history, not in class but in the pages of *Gone with the Wind* and *The Young Lions,* just as an even earlier generation was swept up and carried back in time by *Ben Hur*. The first book I ever loved throbbed with the turning wheel of a long-vanished riverboat plying the nineteenth century.

"Shotgun Cheatham's Last Night Above Ground" is set in 1929. "The Electric Summer" goes to the great world's fair of 1904. Blossom Culp displays her Special Powers during the 1910 school year. "By Far the Worst Pupil at Long Point School" is set in that timeless territory, the recollections of old folks.

Three of these stories have something else in common. They all relate somehow to my novels. My first story, "Priscilla and the Wimps," had taught me how a short story can inspire a novel. I found I liked Priscilla and Melvin and wanted to see more of them. I wanted to learn how the friendship between the largest girl in school and the smallest boy would work out. They therefore reappear as Teresa and Barnie in a novel called *Secrets of the Shopping Mall* that had a long and happy life of its own, in several languages.

"Shotgun Cheatham's Last Night Above Ground" has had a happier history still, from even less likely beginnings. It started when author Harry Mazer sent out a letter to his writing friends in 1995. He wanted, of all things, gun stories for a collection that came to be *Twelve Shots*. Even before Columbine, this didn't seem a promising project to me. But Harry thought the controversial gun topic would stimulate a bracing range of writerly response.

I wondered. It seemed to me he was apt to get too many terminally gritty, male-dominated, testosterone-tainted tales—all grim. For balance, I thought I'd try a comedy starring a female character. It was the assignment I gave myself. Harry provided the necessary deadline.

This is how Grandma Dowdel came to be—and to seize control of my career. When the editor of my novels read this short story, she told me to write some more short stories this grandson, Joey, tells about his grandma, and to shape them into a novel told in stories.

The result was *A Long Way from Chicago*. It was a National Book Award finalist in 1998. It won the John Newbery silver medal from the American Library Association in 1999. When these things happen, your editors say, "We'll need a sequel," and again, they'd like it by Thursday. That second book became *A Year Down Yonder,* the John Newbery gold medal winner in 2001 . . . a pair of ascending Newberys, and all because a writing colleague asked me to write a gun story. I scanned the mail daily for my next assignment.

Along it came in a letter from the well-known anthologist Donald R. Gallo. He wanted short stories from ten young-adult writers, one story for each decade of the twentieth century for a collection that became *Time Capsule.*

Somehow I was assigned the 1900–10 decade for the setting of my story. (Or did I ask for this decade so mine could be the first story? Surely not.) The signal event of that decade, to me, was the great Louisiana Purchase Exposition, the world's fair of 1904 in St. Louis. An Illinois farm girl named Geneva Peck had brought a ruby-glass cup etched with "1904" from the fair to her little brother, who became my father. Not for the first time did I mine the memories of my elders for a story.

In "The Electric Summer" a farm girl who's never been anywhere sees the great world suddenly unfold before her at the fair. What ideal metaphors for finding your future were world's fairs in their heydays: electrically lit epiphanies.

A short story couldn't begin to explore the possibilities. So was born a novel called *Fair Weather* about a farm family of kids who find their twentieth-century futures at another fair, the World's Columbian Exposition in the Chicago of 1893.

A grateful *Chicago Tribune* gave the book the paper's first annual young-adult novel prize in 2002. All because of a short story.

The history of "The Special Powers of Blossom Culp" is a tale told in reverse. When Johanna Hurwitz sent out her call, she wanted an entire collection of stories, *Birthday Surprises,* to explore the same odd idea: A child receives a handsomely wrapped box with nothing in it.

Somehow this brought Blossom Culp to mind. Through four books of my early career she'd become my most popular character: the poorest, plainest, least truthful pupil at Horace Mann School. From Blossom I'd learned that young readers will identify most lovingly with exactly the kind of people they wouldn't sit next to in school.

Blossom lives by her wits. Being an outcast, a peer-group pariah, she has nothing to lose and is therefore the freest spirit in Bluff City.

The empty-gift-box motif of the collection seemed just right for a prequel to the four novels that start with *The Ghost Belonged to Me* a little later in Blossom's busy career. The short story dramatizes the lasting first impression she makes when she and her eerie mama blow into town.

The last story in this section, "By Far the Worst Pupil at Long Point School," is one of the most recently written. But it has a long family history. My mother was a student (never a teacher) at a one-room schoolhouse in rural Morgan County, Illinois, called Long Point School. And so that's the name of the school in this story with a surprise at the end.

My mother, who was a first grader in 1912, recalled riding a horse to Long Point School. A picture hangs in my mind of her and two of her older brothers astride a big farm horse, clopping down the dirt road, my mother the small figure behind with the big bow at the back of her head. Very likely there's a story waiting to be told about these three.

The Electric Summer

I was sitting out there on the old swing that used to hang on the back porch. We'd fed Dad and the boys. Now Mama and I were spelling each other to stir the preserves. The screen door behind me was black with flies, and that smell of sugared strawberries cooking down filled all out-of-doors. A Maytime smell, promising summer.

Just turned fourteen, I was long-legged enough to push off the swing, then listen to the squeak of the chains. The swing was where I did my daytime dreaming. I sat there looking down past Mama's garden and the windpump to the level line of long distance.

Like watching had made it happen, dust rose on the road from town. A black dot got bigger, scaring the sheep away from the fence line. It was an automobile. Nothing else churned the dust like that. Then by and by it was the Schumates' Oldsmobile turning off the crown of the road and bouncing into our barn lot. There were only four automobiles in the town at that time, and only one of them driven by a woman—my aunt Elvera Schumate. She cut the motor off, but the Oldsmobile was still heaving. Climbing down, she put a gloved hand on a fender to calm it.

As Dad often said, Aunt Elvera would have been a novelty even without the automobile. In the heat of the day she wore a wide-brimmed canvas hat secured with a motoring veil tied under her chin. Her duster was a voluminous poplin garment, leather-bound at the hem.

My cousin Dorothy climbed down from the Olds, dressed similarly. They made a business of untangling themselves from their veils, propping their goggles up on their foreheads, and dusting themselves down the best they could. Aunt Elvera made for the house with Dorothy following. Dorothy always held back.

Behind me Mama banged the screen door to scare the flies, then stepped outside. She was ready for a breather even if it meant Aunt Elvera. I stood up from the swing as she came through the gate to the yard, Dorothy trailing. Where their goggles had been were two circles of clean skin around their eyes. They looked like a pair of raccoons. Mama's mouth twitched in something of a smile.

"Well, Mary." Aunt Elvera heaved herself up the porch steps and drew off the gauntlet gloves. "I can see you are having a busy day." Mama's hands were fire red from strawberry juice and the heat of the stove. Mine were scratched all over from picking every ripe berry in the patch.

"One day's like another on the farm," Mama remarked.

"Then I will not mince words," Aunt Elvera said, overlooking me. "I'd have rung you up if you were on the telephone."

"What about, Elvera?" She and Mama weren't sisters. They were sisters-in-law.

"Why, the Fair, of course!" Aunt Elvera bristled in an important way. "What else? The Louisiana Purchase Exposition in St. Louis. The world will be there. It puts St. Louis at the hub of the universe." Aunt Elvera's mouth worked.

"Well I do know," Mama said. "I take it you'll be going?"

Aunt Elvera waved her away. "My stars, yes. You know how Schumate can be. Tight as a new boot. But I put my foot down. Mary, this is the opportunity of a lifetime. We will not see such wonders again during our span."

"Ah," Mama said, and my mind wandered—took a giant leap and landed in St. Louis. We knew about the Fair. The calendar the peddler gave us at Christmas featured a different pictorial view of the Fair for every month. They were white palaces in gardens with gondolas in waterways, everything electric lit. Castles from Europe and paper houses from Japan. For the month of May the calendar featured the great floral clock on the fairgrounds.

"Send us a postal," Mama said.

"The thing is . . ." Aunt Elvera's eyes slid toward Dorothy. "We thought we'd invite Geneva to go with us."

My heart liked to lurch out of my apron. Me? They wanted to take me to the Fair?

"She'll be company for Dorothy."

Then I saw how it was. Dorothy was dim, but she could set her heels like a mule. She wanted somebody with her at the Fair so she wouldn't have to trail after her mother every minute. We were about the same age. We were in the same grade, but she was a year older, having repeated fourth grade. She could read, but her lips moved. And we were cousins, not friends.

"It will be educational for them both," Aunt Elvera said. "All the progress of civilization as we know it will be on display. They say a visit to the Fair is tantamount to a year of high school."

"Mercy," Mama said.

"We will take the Wabash Railroad directly to the gates of the Exposition," Aunt Elvera explained, "and we will be staying on the grounds themselves at the Inside Inn." She leaned nearer Mama, and her voice fell. "I'm sorry to say that there will be stimulants for sale on the fairgrounds. You know how St. Louis is in the hands of the breweries." Aunt Elvera was sergeant-at-arms of the Women's Christian Temperance Union, and to her, strong drink was a mocker. "But we will keep the girls away from that sort of thing." Her voice fell to a whisper. "And we naturally won't set foot on The Pike."

We knew what The Pike was. It was the midway of the Fair, like a giant carnival with all sorts of goings-on.

"Well, many thanks, but I don't think so," Mama said.

My heart didn't exactly sink. It never dawned on me that I'd see the Fair. I was only a little cast down because I might never get another glimpse of the world.

"Now, you're not to think of the money," Aunt Elvera said. "Dismiss that from your mind. Schumate and I will be glad to cover all Geneva's expenses. She can sleep in the bed with Dorothy, and we are carrying a good deal of our eats. I know these isn't flush times for farmers, Mary, but do not let your pride stand in Geneva's way."

"Oh no," Mama said mildly. "Pride cometh before a fall. But we may be running down to the Fair ourselves."

Aunt Elvera's eyes narrowed, and I didn't believe Mama either. It was just her way of fending off my aunt. Kept me from being in the same bed with Dorothy too.

Aunt Elvera never liked taking no for an answer, but in time she and Dorothy made a disorderly retreat. We saw them off from the porch. Aunt Elvera had to crank the Olds to get it going while Dorothy sat up on the seat, adjusting the magneto or whatever it was. We watched Aunt Elvera's rear elevation as she stooped to jerk the crank time after time. If the crank got away from you, it could break your arm, and we watched to see if it would.

But at length the Olds coughed and sputtered to life. Aunt Elvera climbed aboard and circled the barn lot—she never had found the reverse gear. Then they were off back to town in a cloud of dust on the crown of the road.

I didn't want to mention the Fair, so I said, "Mama, would you ride in one of them things?"

"Not with Elvera running it," she said, and went back in the house.

I could tell you very little about the rest of that day. My mind was miles off. I know Mama wrung the neck off a fryer, and we had baking-powder biscuits to go with the warm jam. After supper my brothers hitched up Fanny to the trap and went into town. I took a bottle brush to the lamp chimneys and trimmed the wicks. After that I was back out on the porch swing while there was some daylight left. The lightning bugs were coming out, so that reminded me of how the Fair was lit up at night with electricity, brighter than day.

Then Mama came out and settled in the swing beside me. She never sat out until the nights got hotter than this. We swung together awhile. Then she said in a quiet voice, "I meant it. I want you to see the Fair."

Everything stopped then. I still didn't believe it, but my heart turned over.

"I spoke to your dad about it. He can't get away, and he can't spare the boys. But I want us to go to the Fair."

Oh, she was brave to say it, she who hadn't been any-where in her life. Brave even to think it. "I've got some egg money put back," she said. We didn't keep enough chickens to sell the eggs, but anything you managed to save was called egg money.

"That's for a rainy day," I said, being practical.

"I know it," she said. "But I'd like to see that floral clock." Mama was famous for her garden flowers. When her glads were up, every color, people drove by to see them. And there was nobody to touch her for her zinnias.

Oh, Mama, I thought, is this just a game we're playing? "What'll we wear?" I asked, to test her.

"They'll be dressy down at the Fair, won't they?" she said. "You know those artificial cornflowers I've got. I thought I'd trim my hat with them. And you're getting to be a big girl. Time you had a corset."

So then I knew she meant business.

That's how Mama and I went to the Louisiana Purchase Exposition in St. Louis, that summer of 1904. We studied up on it, and dad read the Fair literature along with us. Hayseeds we might be, but we meant to be informed hayseeds. They said the Fair covered twelve hundred acres, and we tried to see that in our minds, how many farms that would amount to. And all we learned about the Fair filled my heart to overflowing and struck me dumb with dread.

Mama weakened some. She found out when the Schumates were going, and we planned to go at the same time, just so we'd know somebody there. But we didn't take the same train.

When the great day came, Dad drove us to town where the Wabash Cannonball stopped on its way to St. Louis. If he'd turned the trap around and taken us back home, you wouldn't have heard a peep out of me. And I think Mama was the same. But then we were on the platform with the big locomotive thundering in, everything too quick now, and too loud.

We had to scramble for seats in the day coach, lugging one straw valise between us and a gallon jug of lemonade. And a thermos bottle of the kind the Spanish-American War soldiers carried, with our own well water for brushing our teeth. We'd heard that St. Louis water comes straight out of the Mississippi River, and there's enough silt in it to settle at the bottom of the glass. We'd go to their fair, but we weren't going to drink their water.

When the people sitting across from us went to the dining car, Mama and I spread checkered napkins over our knees and had our noon meal out of the hamper. All the while, hot wind blew clinkers and soot in the window as we raced along like a crazed horse. Then a lady flounced up and perched on the seat opposite. She had a full bird on the wing sewn to the crown of her hat, and she was painted up like a circus pony, so we took her to be from Chicago. Leaning forward, she spoke, though we didn't know her from Adam. "Would you know where the ladies' restroom is?" she inquired.

We stared blankly back, but then Mama said, politely, "No, but you're welcome to rest here till them other people come back."

The woman blinked at us, then darted away, hurrying now. I chewed on that a minute, along with my ham sandwich.

Then I said, "Mama, do you suppose they have a privy on the train?"

"A *what?*" she said.

Finally, we had to know. Putting the valise on my seat and the hamper on hers, Mama and I went to explore. We walked through the swaying cars, from seat to seat, the cornflowers on Mama's hat aquiver. Sure enough, we came to a door at the end of a car with a sign reading: LADIES. We crowded inside, and there it was. A water closet like you'd find in town and a chain hanging down and a roll of paper. "Well, I've seen everything now," Mama said. "You wouldn't catch me sitting on that thing in a moving train. I'd fall off."

But I wanted to know how it worked and reached for the handle on the chain. "Just give it a little jerk," Mama said.

We stared down as I did, and the bottom of the pan was on a hinge. It dropped open, and there below were the ties of the Wabash tracks racing along in reverse beneath us.

We both jumped back and hit the door. And we made haste back to our seats. I guess we were lucky not to have found the lady with the bird on her hat in there, sitting down.

Then before I was ready, we were crossing the Mississippi River on a high trestle. There was nothing between us and brown water. I put my hand over my eyes, but not before I glimpsed St. Louis on the far bank, sweeping away in the haze of heat as far as the eye could see.

We didn't stay at the Inside Inn. They wanted two dollars a night for a room, three if they fed you. We booked into a rooming house not far from the main gate, where we got a big square room upstairs with two beds for a dollar. It was run by a severe lady, Mrs. Wolfe, with a small, moon-faced son named Thomas clinging to her skirts. The place suited Mama, once she'd pulled down the bedclothes in case of bugs. It didn't matter where we laid our heads as long as it was clean.

We walked to the Fair that afternoon, following the crowds, trying to act like everybody else. Once again I'd have turned back if Mama said to. It wasn't the awful grandeur of the pavilions rising white in the sun. It was all those people. I didn't know there were that many people in the world. They scared me at first, then I couldn't see enough. My eyes began to drink deep.

We took the Intramural electric railroad that ran around the Exposition grounds, making stops. The Fair passed before us, and it didn't take me long to see what I was looking for. It was hard to miss. At the Palace of Transportation stop, I told Mama this was where we got off.

There it rose before us, two hundred and fifty feet high. It was the giant wheel, the invention of George Washington Gale Ferris. A great wheel with thirty-six cars on it, each holding sixty people. It turned as we watched, and people were getting on and off like it was nothing to them.

"No power on earth would get me up in that thing," Mama murmured.

But I opened my hand and showed her the dollar extra Dad had slipped me to ride the wheel. "Dad said it would give us a good view of the Fair," I said in a wobbly voice.

"It would give me a stroke," Mama said. But then she set her jaw. "Your dad is putting me to the test. He thinks I won't do it."

Gathering her skirts, she surged forth to the line of people waiting to ride the wheel.

We wouldn't look up while we waited, but we heard the creaking of all that naked steel. "That is the sound of doom," Mama muttered. Then too soon they were ushering us into a car, and I began to babble out of sheer fear.

"A lady named Mrs. Nicholson rode standing on the roof of one of these cars when the wheel was up at the Chicago fair."

Mama turned on me. "What in the world for?"

"She was a daredevil, I guess."

"She was out of her mind," Mama said.

Now we were inside, and people mobbed the windows as we swooped up. I meant to stand in the middle of our car and watch the floor, but I looked out. Now we were above the roofs and towers of the Fair, a white city unfolding. There was the Grand Basin with the gondolas drifting. There was the mighty Festival Hall. Mama chanced a look.

It was cooler up here. My unforgiving Warner's Rust-Proof Corset had held me in a death grip all day, but you could breathe easier up here. Then we paused, dangling at the top. Now we were at one with the birds, like hawks hovering over the Fair.

"How many windpumps high are we?" Mama pondered. As we began to arch down again, we were both at a window, skinning our eyes to see.

Giddy when we got out, we staggered on solid ground and had to sit down on an ornamental bench. Now Mama was game for anything. "If they didn't want an arm and a leg for the fare," she said, "I'd ride that thing again. Keep the ticket stubs to show your dad we did it."

Braver than before, we walked down The Pike as it was still broad daylight. It was lined with sidewalk cafes by the Streets of Cairo and the Palais du Costume, Hagenbeck's Circus and the Galveston Flood. Because we were parched, we found a table at a place where they served a new drink, tea with ice in it. "How do we know we're not drinking silt?" Mama wondered, but it cooled us off.

As quick as you'd sit down anywhere at the Fair, there'd be entertainment. Where we sat in front of the French Village they had a supple young man named Will Rogers doing rope tricks. And music? Everywhere you turned, and all along The Pike the song the world sang that summer: "Meet me in St. Louis, Louis, meet me at the Fair."

We sat over our tea and watched the passing parade. Some of these people you wouldn't want to meet in a dark alley. Over by the water chutes a gang of rough men waited to glimpse the ankles of women getting out of the boats. But the only thing we saw on The Pike we shouldn't have was Uncle Schumate weaving out of the saloon bar of the Tyrolean Alps.

I can't tell all we saw in our two days at the Fair. We tried to look at things the boys and Dad would want to hear about— the Hall of Mines and Metallurgy and the livestock. We learned a good deal of history: the fourteen female statues to stand for the states of the Louisiana Purchase of 1803, and U. S. Grant's log cabin. But most of what we saw foretold the future. Automobiles and airships and moving pictures.

Our last night was the Fourth of July. Fifty bands played, some of them on horseback. John Philip Sousa, in gold braid and white, conducted his own marches. Lit in every color, the fountains played to this music and the thunder of the fireworks. And the cavalry from the Boer War exhibit rode in formation, carrying torches.

Mama turned away from all the army uniforms, thinking of my brothers, I suppose. But when the lights came on, every tower and minaret picked out with electric bulbs, we saw what this new century would be: all the grandeur of ancient Greece and Rome, lit by lightning. A new century, with the United States of America showing the way. But you'd have to run hard not to be left behind.

We saved the floral clock for our last morning. It lay across a hillside next to the Agriculture Palace, and it was beyond anything. The dial of it was 112 feet across, and each giant hand weighed 2,500 pounds. It was all made of flowers, even the numbers. Each hour garden was a plant that opened at that time of day, beginning with morning glories. We stood there in a rapture, waiting for it to strike the hour.

Then who appeared before us with her Eastman Folding Kodak camera slung around her neck but Aunt Elvera Schumate. To demonstrate her worldliness, she merely nodded like we were all just coming out of church back home. "Well, Mary," she said to Mama, "I guess this clock shames your garden."

Mama dipped her head modestly to show the cornflowers on her hat. "Yes, Elvera," she said. "I am a humbler woman for this experience," and Aunt Elvera didn't quite know what to make of this reply. "Where's Dorothy?" Mama asked innocently.

"That child!" Aunt Elvera said. "I couldn't get her out of the bed at the Inside Inn! She complains of blistered feet. Wait till she has a woman's corns! I am a martyr to mine. I cannot get her interested in the Fair. She got as far as the bust of President Roosevelt sculpted in butter, but then she faded." Aunt Elvera cast me a baleful look as if this was all my fault. "Dorothy is going through a phase."

But there Aunt Elvera was wrong. Dorothy never was much better than that for the rest of her life. Mama didn't inquire into Uncle Schumate's whereabouts. We thought we knew.

On the train ride home we were seasoned travelers, Mama and I. When the candy butcher hawked his wares through our car, we knew to turn our faces away from his prices. We crossed the Mississippi River on that terrible trestle, and after Edwardsville the land settled into flat fields. Looking out, Mama said, "Corn's knee-high by the Fourth of July," because she was thinking ahead to home. "I'll sleep good tonight without those streetcars clanging outside the window."

But they still clanged in my mind, and "The Stars and Stripes Forever" blended with "Meet Me in St. Louis, Louis."

"But, Mama, how can we just go home after all we've seen?"

Thinking that over, she said, "You won't have to, you and the boys. It's your century. It can take you wherever you want to go." Then she reached over and put her hand on mine, a thing she rarely did. "I'll keep you back if I can. But I'll let you go if I must."

That thrilled me, and scared me. The great world seemed to swing wide like the gates of the Fair, and I didn't even have a plan. I hadn't even put up my hair yet. It seemed to me it was time for that, time to jerk that big bow off the braid hanging down my back and put up my hair in a woman's way.

"Maybe in the fall," said Mama, who was turning into a mind-reader as we steamed through the July fields, heading for home.

Shotgun Cheatham's Last Night Above Ground

The first time I ever saw a dead body, it was Shotgun Cheatham. We were staying with our Grandma Dowdel, and it was the best trip by far we ever made to her house. My sister Mary Alice and I visited at Grandma Dowdel's every summer when our folks went up to fish in Wisconsin on Dad's week off.

"They dump us on her is what they do," Mary Alice said. She'd have been about nine the year they buried Shotgun. She didn't like going to Grandma's because you had to go outside to the privy. A big old snaggletoothed tomcat lived in the cobhouse, and as quick as you'd come out of the privy, he'd jump at you. Mary Alice hated that.

I liked going because we went on the train. You could go about anywhere on a train in those days, and I didn't care where a train went as long as I was on it. The tracks cut through the town where Grandma Dowdel lived, and people stood out on their porches to see the train go through. It was a town that size.

Mary Alice said that there was nothing to do and nobody to do it with, so she'd tag after me, though I was three years older and a boy. We'd stroll uptown, which was three brick buildings: the bank, the general merchandise, and The Coffee Pot Cafe where the old saloon had stood. Prohibition was on in those days, so people made beer at home. They still had the tin roofs out over the sidewalk and hitching rails. Most farmers came to town horse-drawn, though there were Fords, and the banker drove a Hupmobile.

But it was a slow place except for the time they buried Shotgun Cheatham. He might have made it unnoticed all the way to the grave except for his name. The county seat newspaper didn't want to run an obituary on anybody called Shotgun, but nobody knew any other name for him. This sparked attention from some of the bigger newspapers. One sent in a stringer to nose around The Coffee Pot Cafe for a human-interest story since it was August, a slow month for news.

The Coffee Pot was where people went to loaf, talk tall, and swap gossip. Mary Alice and I were regulars there, and even we were of some interest because we were kin of Mrs.

Dowdel's, who never set foot in the place. She kept herself to herself, which was uphill work in a town like that.

Mary Alice and I carried the tale home that a suspicious type had come off the train in citified clothes and a stiff straw hat. He stuck out a mile and was asking around about Shotgun Cheatham. And he was taking notes.

Grandma had already heard it on the grapevine that Shotgun was no more, though she wasn't the first person people ran to with news. She wasn't what you'd call a popular woman. Grandpa Dowdel had been well thought of, but he was long gone.

That day she was working tomatoes on the black iron range, and her kitchen was hot enough to steam the calendars off the wall. Her sleeves were turned back, and she had arms on her like a man. When she heard the town was apt to fill up with newspaper reporters, her jaw clenched.

Presently she said, "I'll tell you what that reporter's after. He wants to get the horselaugh on us because he thinks we're nothing but a bunch of hayseeds and no-'count country people. We are, but what business is it of his?"

"Who was Shotgun Cheatham anyway?" Mary Alice asked.

"He was just an old reprobate who lived poor and died broke," Grandma said. "Nobody went near him because he smelled like a polecat. He lived in a chicken coop, and now they'll have to burn it down."

To change the subject she said to me, "Here, you stir these tomatoes, and don't let them stick. I've stood in this heat till I'm half-cooked myself."

I hated it when Grandma gave me kitchen work. I wished it was her day for apple butter. She made that outdoors over an open fire, and she put pennies in the cauldron to keep it from sticking.

"Down at The Coffee Pot they say Shotgun rode with the James boys."

"Which James boys?" Grandma asked.

"Jesse James," I said, "and Frank."

"They wouldn't have had him," she said. "Anyhow, them Jameses was Missouri people."

"They were telling the reporter Shotgun killed a man and went to the penitentiary."

"Several around here done that," Grandma said, "though I don't recall him being out of town any length of time. Who's doing all this talking?"

"A real old, humped-over lady with buck teeth," Mary Alice said.

"Cross-eyed?" Grandma said. "That'd be Effie Wilcox. You think she's ugly now, you should have seen her as a girl. And she'd talk you to death. Her tongue's attached in the middle and flaps at both ends." Grandma was over by the screen door for a breath of air.

"They said he'd notched his gun in six places," I said, pushing my luck. "They said the notches were either for banks he'd robbed or for sheriffs he'd shot."

"Was that Effie again? Never trust an ugly woman. She's got a grudge against the world," said Grandma, who was no oil painting herself. She fetched up a sigh. "I'll tell you how

Shotgun got his name. He wasn't but about ten years old, and he wanted to go out and shoot quail with a bunch of older boys. He couldn't hit a barn wall from the inside, and he had a sty in one eye. They were out there in a pasture without a quail in sight, but Shotgun got all excited being with the big boys. He squeezed off a round and killed a cow. Down she went. If he'd been aiming at her, she'd have died of old age eventually. The boys took the gun off him, not knowing who he'd plug next. That's how he got the name, and it stuck to him like fly-paper. Any girl in town could have outshot him, and that includes me." Grandma jerked a thumb at herself.

She kept a twelve-gauge double-barreled Winchester Model 21 behind the woodbox, but we figured it had been Grandpa Dowdel's for shooting ducks. "And I wasn't no Annie Oakley myself, except with squirrels." Grandma was still at the door, fanning her apron. Then in the same voice she said, "Looks like we got company. Take them tomatoes off the fire."

A stranger was on the porch, and when Mary Alice and I crowded up behind Grandma to see, it was the reporter. He was sharp-faced, and he'd sweated through his hatband.

"What's your business?" Grandma said through screen wire, which was as friendly as she got.

"Ma'am, I'm making inquiries about the late Shotgun Cheatham." He shuffled his feet, wanting to get one of them in the door. Then he mopped up under his hat brim with a silk handkerchief. His Masonic ring had diamond chips in it.

"Who sent you to me?"

"I'm going door-to-door, ma'am. You know how you ladies like to talk. Bless your hearts, you'd all talk the hind leg off a mule."

Mary Alice and I both stared at that. We figured Grandma would grab up her broom to swat him off the porch. She could make short work of peddlers even when they weren't lippy. And tramps never marked her fence. But to our surprise she swept open the screen door and stepped out on the back porch. You didn't get inside her house even if you knew her. I followed and so did Mary Alice once she was sure the snaggle-toothed tom wasn't lurking around out there, waiting to pounce.

"You a newspaper reporter?" she said. "Peoria?" It was the flashy clothes, but he looked surprised. "What they been telling you?"

"Looks like I got a good story by the tail," he said. " 'Last of the Old Owlhoot Gunslingers Goes to a Pauper's Grave.' That kind of angle. Ma'am, I wonder if you could help me flesh out the story some."

"Well, I got flesh to spare," Grandma said mildly. "Who's been talking to you?"

"It was mainly an elderly lady—"

"Ugly as sin, calls herself Wilcox?" Grandma said. "She's been in the state hospital for the insane until just here lately, but as a reporter I guess you nosed that out."

Mary Alice nudged me hard, and the reporter's eyes widened.

"They tell you how Shotgun come by his name?"

"Opinions seem to vary, ma'am."

"Ah well, fame is fleeting," Grandma said. "He got it in the Civil War."

The reporter's hand hovered over his breast pocket where a notepad stuck out.

"Oh yes. Shotgun went right through the war with the Illinois Volunteers. Shiloh in the spring of sixty-two, and he was with U. S. Grant when Vicksburg fell. That's where he got his name. Grant give it to him, in fact. Shotgun didn't hold with government-issue firearms. He shot rebels with his old Remington pump-action that he'd used to kill quail back here at home."

Now Mary Alice was yanking on my shirttail. We knew kids lie all the time, but Grandma was no kid, and she could tell some whoppers. Of course the reporter had been lied to big-time up at the cafe, but Grandma's lies were more interesting, even historical. They made Shotgun look better while they left Effie Wilcox in the dust.

"He was always a crack shot," she said, winding down. "Come home from the war with a line of medals bigger than his chest."

"And yet he died penniless," the reporter said in a thoughtful voice.

"Oh well, he'd sold off them medals and give the money to war widows and orphans."

A change crossed the reporter's narrow face. Shotgun had gone from kill-crazy gunslinger to war hero marksman.

Philanthropist, even. He fumbled his notepad out and was scribbling. He thought he'd hit pay dirt with Grandma. "It's all a matter of record," she said. "You could look it up."

He was ready to wire in a new story: "Civil War Hero Handpicked by U. S. Grant called to the Great Campground in the Sky." Something like that. "And he never married?"

"Never did," Grandma said. "He broke Effie Wilcox's heart. She's bitter still, as you see."

"And now he goes to a pauper's grave with none to mark his passing," the reporter said, which may have been a sample of his writing style.

"They tell you that?" Grandma said. "They're pulling your leg, sonny. You drop by The Coffee Pot and tell them you heard that Shotgun's being buried from my house with full honors. He'll spend his last night above ground in my front room, and you're invited."

The reporter backed down the porch stairs, staggering under all this new material. "Much obliged, ma'am."

"Happy to help," Grandma said.

Mary Alice had turned loose of my shirttail. What little we knew about grown-ups never seemed to cover Grandma. She turned on us. "Now I've got to change my shoes and walk all the way up to the lumberyard in this heat," she said, as if she hadn't brought it all on herself. Up at the lumberyard they'd be knocking together Shotgun Cheatham's coffin and sending the bill to the county, and Grandma had to tell them to bring that coffin to her house, with Shotgun in it.

* * *

By nightfall a green pine coffin stood on two sawhorses in the bay window of the front room, and people milled in the yard. They couldn't see Shotgun from there because the coffin lid blocked the view. Besides, a heavy gauze hung from the open lid and down over the front of the coffin to veil him. Shotgun hadn't been exactly fresh when they discovered his body. Grandma had flung open every window, but there was a peculiar smell in the room. I'd only had one look at him when they'd carried in the coffin, and that was enough. I'll tell you just two things about him. He didn't have his teeth in, and he was wearing bib overalls.

The people in the yard still couldn't believe Grandma was holding open house. This didn't stop the reporter, who was haunting the parlor, looking for more flesh to add to his story. And it didn't stop Mrs. L. J. Weidenbach, the banker's wife, who came leading her father, an ancient codger half her size in full Civil War Union Blue.

"We are here to pay our respects at this sad time," Mrs. Weidenbach said when Grandma let them in. "When I told Daddy that Shotgun had been decorated by U. S. Grant and wounded three times at Bull Run, it brought it all back to him, and we had to come." Her old daddy wore a forage cap and a decoration from the Grand Army of the Republic, and he seemed to have no idea where he was. She led him up to the coffin, where they admired the flowers. Grandma had planted a pitcher of glads from her garden at either end of the pine box. In each pitcher she'd stuck an American flag.

A few more people willing to brave Grandma came and went, but finally we were down to the reporter, who'd settled into the best chair, still nosing for news. Then who appeared at the front door but Mrs. Effie Wilcox, in a hat.

"Mrs. Dowdel, I've come to set with you overnight and see our brave old soldier through his Last Watch."

In those days people sat up with a corpse through the final night before burial. I'd have bet money Grandma wouldn't let Mrs. Wilcox in for a quick look, let alone overnight. But of course Grandma was putting on the best show possible to pull wool over the reporter's eyes. Little though she thought of townspeople, she thought less of strangers. Grandma waved Mrs. Wilcox inside, and in she came, stared at the blank white gauze, and said, "Don't he look natural?"

Then she drew up a chair next to the reporter. He flinched because he had it on good authority that she'd just been let out of the insane asylum. "Warm, ain't it?" she said straight at him, but looking everywhere.

The crowd outside finally dispersed. Mary Alice and I hung at the edge of the room, too curious to be anywhere else.

"If you're here for the long haul," Grandma said to the reporter, "how about a beer?" He looked encouraged, and Grandma left him to Mrs. Wilcox, which was meant as a punishment. She came back with three of her home brews, cellar-cool. She brewed beer to drink herself, but these three bottles were to see the reporter through the night. She wouldn't have expected her worst enemy, Effie Wilcox, to drink alcohol in front of a man.

In normal circumstances the family recalls stories about the departed to pass the long night hours. But these circumstances weren't normal, and quite a bit had already been recalled about Shotgun Cheatham anyway.

Only a single lamp burned, and as midnight drew on, the glads drooped in their pitchers. I was wedged in a corner, beginning to doze, and Mary Alice was sound asleep on a throw rug. After the second beer, the reporter lolled, visions of Shotgun's Civil War glories no doubt dancing in his head. You could hear the tick of the kitchen clock. Grandma's chin would drop, then jerk back. Mrs. Wilcox had been humming "Rock of Ages," but tapered off after "let me hide myself in thee."

Then there was the quietest sound you ever heard. Somewhere between a rustle and a whisper. It brought me around, and I saw Grandma sit forward and cock her head. I blinked to make sure I was awake, and the whole world seemed to listen. Not a leaf trembled outside.

But the gauze that hung down over the open coffin moved. Twitched.

Except for Mary Alice, we all saw it. The reporter sat bolt upright, and Mrs. Wilcox made a little sound.

Then nothing.

Then the gauze rippled as if a hand had passed across it from the other side, and in one place it wrinkled into a wad as if somebody had snagged it. As if a feeble hand had reached up from the coffin depths in one last desperate attempt to live before the dirt was shoveled in.

Every hair on my head stood up.

"Naw," Mrs. Wilcox said, strangling. She pulled back in her chair, and her hat went forward. "Naw!"

The reporter had his chair arms in a death grip. "Sweet mother of—"

But Grandma rocketed out of her chair. "Whoa, Shotgun!" she bellowed. "You've had your time, boy. You don't get no more!"

She galloped out of the room faster than I'd ever seen her move. The reporter was riveted, and Mrs. Wilcox was sinking fast.

Quicker than it takes to tell, Grandma was back and already raised to her aproned shoulder was the twelve-gauge Winchester from behind the woodbox. She swung it wildly around the room, skimming Mrs. Wilcox's hat, and took aim at the gauze that draped the yawning coffin. Then she squeezed off a round.

I thought that sound would bring the house down. I couldn't hear right for a week. Then Grandma roared out, "Rest in peace, I tell you, you old—" Then she let fly with the other barrel.

The reporter came out of the chair and whipped completely around in a circle. Beer bottles went everywhere. The straight route to the front door was in Grandma's line of fire, and he didn't have the presence of mind to realize she'd already discharged both barrels. He went out a side window, headfirst, leaving his hat and his notepad behind. Which he feared more, the living dead or Grandma's aim, he didn't tarry to tell. Mrs. Wilcox was on her feet, hollering, "The dead is walking, and

Mrs. Dowdel's gunning for me!" She cut and ran out the door and into the night.

When the screen door snapped to behind her, silence fell. Mary Alice hadn't moved. The first explosion had blasted her awake, but she naturally thought that Grandma had killed her, so she didn't bother to budge. She says the whole experience gave her nightmares for years after.

A burned-powder haze hung in the room, cutting the smell of Shotgun Cheatham. The white gauze was black rags now, and Grandma had blown the lid clear of the coffin. She'd have blown out all three windows in the bay, except they were open. As it was, she'd pitted her woodwork bad and topped the snowball bushes outside. But apart from scattered shot, she hadn't disfigured Shotgun Cheatham any more than he already was.

Grandma stood there savoring the silence. Then she turned toward the kitchen with the twelve-gauge loose in her hand. "Time you kids was in bed," she said as she trudged past us.

Apart from Grandma herself, I was the only one who'd seen her big old snaggletoothed tomcat streak out of the coffin and over the windowsill when she let fire. And I suppose she'd seen him climb in, which gave her ideas. It was the cat, sitting smug on Shotgun Cheatham's breathless chest, who'd batted at the gauze the way a cat will. And he sure lit out the way he'd come when Grandma fired just over his ragged ears, as he'd probably used up eight lives already.

The cat in the coffin gave Grandma Dowdel her chance. She never had any time for Effie Wilcox, whose tongue

flapped at both ends, but she had even less for newspaper reporters who think your business is theirs. Courtesy of the cat,
she'd fired a round, so to speak, in the direction of each.

Though she never gloated, she looked satisfied. It certainly
fleshed out her reputation and gave people new reason to leave
her in peace. The story of Shotgun Cheatham's last night above
ground kept The Coffee Pot Cafe fully engaged for the rest of
that long summer. It was a story that grew in the telling in one
of those little towns where there's always time to ponder all the
different kinds of truth.

The Special Powers of
Blossom Culp

My name is Blossom Culp, and I'm ten years old, to the best of my mama's recollection.

I call 1900 the year of my birth, but Mama claims to have no idea of the day. Mama doesn't hold with birthdays. She says they make her feel old. This also saves her giving me a present. You could go through the courthouse down at Sikeston, Missouri, with a fine-tooth comb without turning up my records. But I must have been born because here I am.

Since Mama is hard to overlook, I will just mention her

now. She doesn't know her birthday either but claims to be twenty-nine years old. She has only three teeth in her head, but they are up front, so they make a good showing. Her inky hair flows over her bent shoulders and far down her back. Whenever she appeared in daylight down at Sikeston, horses reared. Mama is a sight.

But she's a woman of wisdom and wonderful when it comes to root mixtures, forbidden knowledge, and other people's poultry. We could live off the land, though the trouble is, it's always somebody else's land. Like many of nature's creatures, Mama goes about her work at night. Get your corn in early, or Mama will have our share. Plant your tomatoes up by the house, or Mama will take them off you by the bushel. She likes her eggs fresh too.

A moonless night suits her best; then off she goes down the hedgerows with a croaker sack flung over her humped shoulder. But nobody's ever caught her. "I can outrun a dawg," says Mama.

It was another of her talents that got us chased out of Sikeston. To hear her tell it, Mama has the Second Sight. For ready money she'll tell your fortune, find lost articles, see through walls, and call up the departed. She can read tea leaves, a pack of cards, your palm, a crystal ball. It doesn't matter to Mama. But because Sikeston was a backward place and narrow in its thinking, her profession was against the law. So her and me had to hotfoot it out of town two jumps ahead of a sheriff's posse.

Mama said that fate was leading her to our next home place. But we'd have hopped a freight in any direction. Aboard a swaying cattle car, Mama grew thoughtful and pulled on her long chin.

"The farther north we get," she said, "the more progressive. Wherever we light, you'll be goin' to school." She shifted a plug of Bull Durham from one cheek to the other. If Mama had ever been to school herself, she'd have mentioned it. About all she can read is tea leaves.

"I been to school before, Mama," I reminded her. Down at Sikeston, I'd dropped into the grade school occasionally. Though when I dropped out again, I wasn't missed.

"I mean you'll be goin' to school regular," Mama said. "I won't have the law on me—believe it."

So when at last we came to rest at the town of Bluff City, I knew school was in my future without even a glimpse into Mama's crystal ball. I well recall the day I strolled into the Horace Mann School in Bluff City, wearing the same duds from when me and Mama had dropped off a cattle car of the Wabash Railroad.

"Yewww," said many of the girls in the school yard, giving me a wide berth. It was no better inside. I was sent to the principal before I had time to break a rule. She was a woman tall as a tree named Miss Mae Spaulding.

"Oh, dear," she said, looking down at me, "we're going to have to find you a comb."

I was small for ten but old for my years. Miss Spaulding grasped this and assigned me to fourth grade. She took me there herself, shooing me on ahead like a chicken. The teacher, name of Miss Cartwright, took a gander at me and said, "Oh, my stars."

"Perhaps you'd have a spare handkerchief to loan Blossom," the principal said to Miss Cartwright over my head.

I wiped my nose on my sleeve and noticed all the eyes of the fourth grade were boring holes in me. The boys' eyes were round with amazement. The girls' eyes were mean slits.

"I guess we had better find Blossom a seat," Miss Cartwright said as Miss Spaulding beat a hasty retreat.

A big girl reared up out of her desk. She wore a bow the size of a kite on the back of her head. "She'll not be sitting next to me!" she sang out, and flopped back.

Her name turned out to be Letty Shambaugh, and once again I didn't need Mama's Second Sight to see I had met an enemy for life.

Miss Cartwright cleared her throat and said, "Boys and girls, we have a new class member. I will ask her to introduce herself."

I looked out across the fourth grade, and they seemed capable of anything. Still, I stood my ground. "My name is Blossom Culp, and I hail from down at Sikeston, Missouri."

"Hillbillies," Letty Shambaugh hissed to the girls around her, "or worse."

"Me and Mama have relocated to Bluff City on account of her business."

"And what is your mother's business?" Miss Cartwright inquired.

"Oh, well, shoot," I says, "Mama is well known for her herbal cures and fortune-telling. She can heal warts too. There's gypsy blood in our family."

Letty Shambaugh smirked. "Ah," says Miss Cartwright. "Are you an only child, Blossom?"

"I am now," I said. "I was born one-half of a pair of Siamese twins, but my twin had to be hacked off my side so I alone could live."

"She lies!" Letty Shambaugh called out, though all the boys were interested in my story.

Miss Cartwright had now pulled back to the blackboard and seemed to cling to the chalk tray. "You may take your seat, Blossom." She pointed to the rear of the room.

I didn't mind it on the back row. But as the weeks passed, the novelty of going to school wore thin. My reading wasn't up to fourth-grade standard either. Still, when we had to rise and read aloud from a library book, I did well. Holding a book up, I'd tell a story I thought of on the spot.

"Lies, lies," Letty would announce, "nothing but lies!" Still, Miss Cartwright was often so fascinated, she didn't stop me.

Then one day she told us that Letty would be having her birthday party on school time. "It is not usual to have a birthday party in class," Miss Cartwright said, "but we are making an exception of Letty."

People were always making an exception of Letty. Her paw was the president of the Board of Education. "Mrs. Shambaugh has very kindly offered to provide a cake," Miss Cartwright said, "and ice-cream punch."

At recess I was in the girls' restroom, which has partitions for modesty. From my stall I eavesdropped on Letty talking to the bunch of girls she rules: Tess and Bess, the Beasley twins; Nola Nirider; and Maisie Markham.

"Now shut up and listen," Letty told them. "I am looking for some first-rate presents from you-all for my birthday. Don't get me any of that five-and-dime stuff."

I was so interested in Letty's commandments that I leaned on the door of my stall and staggered out into full view.

"Oh, there you are, Blossom," Letty sniffed. "Since you do nothing but tell lies and snoop, I'll thank you not to give me a present at all. You are a poor girl and can't afford it. Besides, I want nothing from the likes of you."

The bell rang, and they all flounced off like a gaggle of geese. But Letty turned back to fire a final warning at me. "And don't let me catch you spying on us again, Blossom!"

You won't, I said, but only to myself.

I sat up that night, waiting for Mama to come home. We'd taken up residence in an abandoned structure over past the streetcar tracks. It must have been midnight before Mama came in and eased her croaker sack down.

Then she busied herself shaking out everything she'd harvested from nearby gardens. From the look of some of it, she'd detoured past the dump. It was late in the season, so all there was to eat was a handful of pale parsnips.

"Well, Mama, I've got me a problem," I told her. "A stuck-up girl at school is having a birthday party, and I mean to give her a present like anybody else."

Mama surveyed her night's haul. "See anything here you can use?"

She held up a lady's whalebone corset straight off the trash heap and busted beyond repair. Besides, it wouldn't go halfway around Letty. The rest of the stuff was worse, except for a nice hatbox only a little dented with the tissue paper still inside. When I reached for it, Mama only shrugged, and picked between two of her three teeth.

The school days droned on, but I kept my wits about me. In one of my read-alouds, I went too far. Holding up a library copy of *Rebecca of Sunnybrook Farm,* I told the class about the time Mama came across the severed head of a woman and how Mama could identify the murderer with her Second Sight.

"A pack of lies!" Letty bawled out. "And disgusting!"

"That will do, Blossom," Miss Cartwright said in a weary voice. So after that, I had little to occupy myself with but to lie low and snoop on other people's business.

On the afternoon of Letty's party, a cake was wheeled in as large and pink as Letty herself. The classroom was stacked with tastefully wrapped presents, and no learning was done that afternoon. Miss Cartwright hung at the edge while Letty was the center of attention, where she likes to be.

We played some games too childish to interest me, but I managed three slabs of cake and copped an extra slice for Mama. Then it was time for the presents.

"Oh heavens, you shouldn't have!" says Letty, her pudgy fingers fluttering over the vast heap. "Land sakes, I don't know which one to open first!"

"Start with this one." I nudged the hatbox toward her with the toe of my shoe. I'd dressed it up with a bow I found in the school yard and some gold star stickers I'd come across in a teacher's desk.

Miss Cartwright was standing by. Though strict, she sometimes eyed me sympathetically, though it might only have been pity. "Yes, Letty," she said. "Start with Blossom's present."

So Letty had to. She shook the box but heard nothing. She lifted the lid and ran a hand through the tissue paper. "But there's nothing in it," she gasped, shooting me a dangerous look.

Some of the boys snickered, but the girls just pursed up their lips. "Oh, dear," Miss Cartwright remarked. Now Letty had turned the hatbox upside down. The tissue paper dropped out and with it a small note I'd hand-lettered. She read it aloud:

> *To Letty,*
> *Since I am too poor to buy you a present, I will*
> *share with you my own personal Gift.*
> *Believe it.*
> *Blossom Culp*

Letty glanced longingly at her other presents. "What is this so-called personal Gift of yours, Blossom?"

"Just a little demonstration of the Special Powers I inherited from my mama," I replied.

Letty shook a fist at me. "Blossom, you aren't going to ruin my party by showing off and telling lies!"

"For example," I said, cool as a cucumber, "before you even open up your other presents, I can tell what's in them with my Inner Eye. It's a Gift, and I have it down pat."

The girls were fixing to turn on me, but a boy said, "Then do it."

I could read the card on Nola Nirider's. "Now, you take Nola's present." I pointed it out. "No, I don't want to touch it. Just give me a minute." I let my head loll. Then I let my eyes roll back in my head. It was a ghastly sight, and the class gasped. In a voice faint and far-off I said, "Within the wrappings, I see . . . a woman! She is a dainty creature cut in two at the waist!" I let my eyes roll back in place and looked around. "What did I say?"

Letty was already tearing open Nola's present. She pulled out a dainty china powder box in the shape of a lady. It was in two parts. The lid was the upper half. The boys blinked, and the girls looked worried.

Reading the card on Maisie's present from afar, I said, "Now, you take that one from Maisie Markham." And back flipped my eyes, and my head bobbed around till it like to fall off. "Deep within that fancy package," I moaned weirdly, "is a sealed bottle of apple-blossom toilet water—retailing at seventy-nine cents. I sense it with my Inner Nose."

Letty ripped open the box, coming up with that selfsame bottle of toilet water. "How am I doin'?" I asked the class.

It was like that with Tess's brush-and-comb set and Bess's four hair ribbons in rainbow hues. My eyes rolled back so often, showing my whites, that I thought I'd never get them straight in their sockets.

By now Letty sat sprawled in a heap of wrapping paper. The tears streamed down her red face. She was clouding up and ready to squall and had to stand to stamp her foot. "You have ruined my party with your showing off, Blossom. I knew you would, and you have!" She pounded out of the room before she even got to any presents from the boys, which was just as well. The other girls followed her as usual.

Now I was left with the boys, who showed me new respect, unsure of my Special Powers. But then the bell rang, and they trooped out, taking final swipes at the remains of the cake.

"One moment, Blossom," Miss Cartwright said before I could make it to the door. "Could it be as you say—that you have . . . unearthly powers? Or could it merely be that you eavesdropped in the restroom often enough to hear those girls telling each other what they were giving Letty—and then you added that business with your eyes?"

Her chalky hand rested on my shoulder. "No, don't tell me," she said. "I don't want to know."

I was ready to cut out, but Miss Cartwright continued. "It has not taken you long to make a name for yourself at Horace Mann School. You will never be popular. But I have hopes for your future, Blossom. You will go far in your own peculiar way."

And I only nodded, as it's never wise to disagree with a teacher. Then she turned me loose, and I went on my way.

By Far the Worst Pupil
at Long Point School

When we were kids, we always ate our Christmas dinner at
Grandma and Grandpa's, who I though had been around since
the Ice Age. They lived in that little frame house back in the
fields past Long Point School. Of course house and school are
long vanished now, gone to wherever memories go.

Grandma could do some cooking once she got that old iron
stove fired up. Come Christmas day, every chair around her
table was filled. Uncle Billy never missed. Being a bachelor, he
made the rounds of other people's tables for all his holiday

meals and most Sunday dinners. "He can smell a turkey roasting from the other end of the county," Grandma said.

Some people welcomed Uncle Billy for the stories he told. Other people put up with him. Grandma put up with him. She was his big sister, though a quarter his size.

Since Uncle Billy had never married or left the district, nothing had happened to him as a grown-up. All his stories were about the days of yore when he was a boy. Trying to picture Uncle Billy and Grandpa and Grandma as young was more than I could manage. They all three looked to me like they'd been whittled out of used lumber.

Uncle Billy was full of stories, but a lot of us grandkids had never heard Grandpa speak. Certain people claimed the last words Grandpa ever uttered were at his wedding to Grandma when he said, "I do."

"Who wants more oyster dressing?" Grandma said.

"I do!" Uncle Billy said, which made us all look at him, then at Grandpa. Grandpa blinked.

"Who besides Billy?" said Grandma from the kitchen door.

After the turkey and trimmings came the pies and the suet pudding with hard sauce, and finally a bowl of fruit nobody touched. Only then did Uncle Billy ease back from the table. When he undid the top button on his pants and the last button of his vest, we knew we were in for a story.

He said all his stories were to benefit us young ones. He put them together like quilts, with scenes from earlier tales stitched into new patterns. "Oh, you talk about strict," he said, letting out another button. "You don't know what strict is, without my sister for your teacher."

He glanced at Grandma, who said, "It wasn't any picnic for me either, and for eight dollars a month."

We'd heard about how Grandma had been the teacher at Long Point School when she was still only a teenaged girl herself.

"I'd just put my toe over the line a very little bit," said Billy, "and she'd come down on me like the wolf on the fold."

"You couldn't help being a slow thinker, Billy," Grandma observed, "but the least you could do was behave."

"She like to wear me out with that paddle. It hung on the wall right there within her reach. Oh, she was quick with that paddle! I couldn't sit all the way down without pain until I was right at thirty years of age."

"I thought it would take you that long to get through eighth grade," Grandma remarked.

"She'd even whup a girl if that girl got sassy with her. She whupped Gladys Birdwell."

Grandma never really reminisced, but now she nodded. "I have an idea there are still marks on Gladys that don't show in daylight."

"She'd paddle a boy half again her size," Uncle Billy recalled. "But of course it didn't work with Charlie. Nothing fazed Charlie. He was by far the worst pupil at Long Point School."

Grandma sat with us now, around the remains of Christmas dinner. "No," she admitted, "the paddle didn't work on Charlie."

"We had us two privies," Uncle Billy explained. "One for the boys, one for the girls."

We young ones watched the buttons on his straining vest. After such a meal if one of those buttons popped off, it could put your eye out.

"And Charlie was sweet on some girl. Was it Gladys Birdwell?"

"It was Estelle Grub," Grandma said.

"Anyway, Charlie's notion of getting a girl's attention was to steal her stocking cap and throw it down the girls' privy. Just the idea of a boy going into the girls' privy was enough to call out the National Guard at that time. But would that faze Charlie? No. This was at recess, and somebody run to tell teacher on him."

"It was you, Billy," Grandma said.

"And that sister of mine bust out of Long Point Schoolhouse like she was being shot from a cannon. Her boots never touched gravel as she rounded the building. And in her hand, a padlock and a—"

"No, Billy. You got two different stories mixed up in your head," Grandma said, "as usual."

Uncle Billy looked hurt.

"This isn't the padlock story," Grandma said. "This is the fishing-pole story. When Charlie threw Estelle's stocking cap down the privy, I made him take a bamboo pole and a hook and line and go fishing for it down the privy hole. Took him nearly till dark to snag that stocking cap."

"Did it faze Charlie?" one of us grandkids asked.

"Not much," Grandma said, "even when I made him wear the cap. The padlock story took place the following year when Charlie was repeating eighth grade."

"That's right," Uncle Billy said, hoping to tell it. "We always locked both them privies every night to discourage vandals and trespassers. The padlocks theirselves rested in teacher's desk all day long.

"Well, sir, one day at recess Charlie not only went back to the girls' privy, but he was smoking in there. You could see the smoke curling out of the half-moon cut in the privy door. And naturally no girl could use it. Somebody run to teacher to tell on—"

"It was you, Billy," Grandma said.

"And that sister of mine bust out of Long Point Schoolhouse like she was being shot from a cannon. Her boots never touched gravel as she rounded the building. And in her hand, a padlock and a claw hammer and a chunk of wood, and in her mouth two tenpenny nails.

"She drew up short at the girls' privy and snapped the padlock on the latch. That hemmed in Charlie right there. Then she put that chunk of wood up against the half-moon cut in the door and drove the nails in to keep it in place. She meant to smoke that boy like a turkey.

"She was quick, so I have an idea Charlie didn't grasp what had happened and kept on smoking. But it had to dawn on him that there was less and less air to breathe in there, though no privy's airtight. Anyway, when he tried the door, he seen he was in jail. By then teacher was ringing the bell to call us back from recess. But it was hard to concentrate on our lessons the rest of that morning."

"Concentration never came easy for you, Billy," Grandma said.

"The sounds coming from the girls' privy would have waked up the dead," Uncle Billy remembered. "Charlie was like a bull kicking in a pen. It was cold weather, so he had on boots, and he commenced kicking all four sides. It took him till noon, but he knocked that privy down. Finally it was just Charlie standing out there on bald ground, breathing hard. The privy door was flat before him, and the landscape was littered with pages from the Sears catalogue fluttering like moths."

"And there is but little justice in this world," Grandma added. "The School Board took the cost of that privy out of my wages. They said I'd overstepped my bounds, that I was hired to educate my pupils, not to cure them like hams."

"But did it faze Charlie?" one of us grandkids wondered.

"Not in the least," Grandma said.

"There was only one thing left to be done," Uncle Billy said.

"And I did it," Grandma said.

"What?" we grandkids chorused.

"I married him," Grandma said. She peered down the table at Grandpa. "Remember that, Charlie?"

"I do," Grandpa said.

The Supernatural

You're never alone in the dark.
Or if you are, you can't be sure.
—"Shadows"

These next stories stand in the middle of the book, between the
tales of the past and a third group to come set in the present or
at least recent times. "Girl at the Window," "The Most Important Night of Melanie's Life," "Waiting for Sebastian," and
"Shadows" are all supernatural, or flavored with the supernatural. They fall in the center because the supernatural so often
shifts the shape of time, blending the past with the present.

Think of Charles Dickens's *A Christmas Carol*. After all, ghosts are time travelers, and they have the ability to reset our clocks.

But do I believe in them? Not really, and may I never see one. But what would the history of literature, of storytelling, be without ghosts? From the Bible to the first scene of *Hamlet,* to the countless yarns spun in a continuous skein around flickering campfires, they make us edge a little nearer the firelight, and each other.

None of the ghosts in my stories derive from actual sightings, but all the settings are real places. That's what all fiction is to me: what might be in settings that are.

Once, I flew to Emporia, Kansas, sitting next to the pilot in a single-engine plane with a defective door. We flew so low over the country towns that I could read the water towers. Thus, the town in "Girl at the Window." "The Most Important Night of Melanie's Life" could be any suburban town far enough north in North America to have a winter.

"Waiting for Sebastian" acknowledges England's grand tradition of the ghost story and the haunted house. The old stately home built for a family that now takes paying guests in the story is a house called Rydal Hall near Grasmere in the English Lake District. You could go there and stay in it yourself. "Shadows" is set upstairs in another stately home in a different clime, along the River Road in south Louisiana. The story mentions a house named Nottoway, and so the setting might be near—very near.

But I'd better say no more about these stories, for fear of giving too much away.

Early in my career, I wouldn't have thought of writing chiller tales of the Unexplained. But I kept getting letters, most of them from boys in the seventh and eighth grades. They asked me where my "weird stuff" was, and my ghost stories. "Ever read any Stephen King?" they inquired helpfully. "R. L. Stine?"

As a matter of fact, I hadn't. But I was working on a novel at the time taking place back in 1912, about a boy and his great-uncle Miles. It was set in the oldest, grandest, eeriest house in my hometown of Decatur, Illinois. Because of the nudging letters (and because the story wasn't going too well), I put a ghost in the novel. The minute this dead girl stepped on the stage, the story came alive. I made sure to signal her in the title too: *The Ghost Belonged to Me*. Then I found I needed another girl in the story, a live one to balance the ghost girl. That very lively living girl became Blossom Culp.

On the day the book was published, Walt Disney Productions was waiting with the television contract. I was from then on a believer in the ghost story, if not ghosts. And so here are some, believe them or not . . .

Girl at the Window

"At least you'll have your own room," Mom said. The car windows were down because the air conditioner was busted. About everything we had was busted.

"At least you'll be starting out in junior high, so it'll be new to everybody."

But everybody except me would be coming from the same grade school. Every time Mom said *at least,* things sounded worse.

"At least we'll have a roof over our heads." She geared down and took the off-ramp. We were pulling a U-Haul with everything we had, going back to live in Mom's hometown. It was the middle of nowhere, with a water tower up on stilts and the smallest-size Wal-Mart.

"We won't have to live with your grandma," she said, softer. "We'll have our own place. You'll be the man of the family."

At least she didn't say *at least*.

We had supper at Grandma's that first night. Grandma sighed a lot and wore Keds. "I don't know what kind of work you think you're going to get around here," she said to Mom.

"You want to watch your step, mister," Grandma said to me, "and not fall into bad company."

I slept hard those first nights and walked around town all day. I probably wouldn't have minded falling into bad company, but whenever I saw kids, I crossed the street. I never walked past 7-Eleven. I didn't find any new friends, and Mom couldn't find her old ones. The days were real long here. But after Mom got a job in the grain elevator office, she said, "At least we're settling in."

Our house had renters' furniture in it, a living-room couch and beds. Mom slept in the bedroom downstairs. I took the attic room at the back, and it looked like nobody'd been up there in years. The closet door wouldn't stay shut, and there were more hangers than I needed. A foggy mirror hung over the dresser. A pale triangle on the wall showed where somebody had pinned up a pennant. At the back of one of the drawers was the kind of comb a girl uses. I dragged the bed nearer the window in case a breeze came up in the night.

A trumpet vine had crawled up over the back porch roof and grew across my window. The sun came in through the leaves, and one of these mornings I'd be getting up for school. I was in no hurry.

Just after I was sleeping good one night, something woke me. I didn't know what. I wasn't used to this place yet, the way the walls slanted up and met at the top. At first I thought it was crickets. But I heard something else. Something scraped the drainpipe, a tinny sound. I waited. Something thumped the back porch roof. I wanted it to be a squirrel. I wanted that real bad.

A scratchy sound came from the window screen. Finger-nails. Long fingernails. I felt them scratching across my brain. I listened so hard, I heard breathing. And it wasn't mine.

No way was I going to look at that window. But I felt my head turning. Sometimes at night the leaves rustled at the win-dow. But I didn't see leaves. A shape was there, filling up the window. A hand was on the screen, and a face pressed against it. The other hand was scuttling around, trying to pull out the bottom of the screen.

I wanted to yell. I wanted to cry.

But now I was on my feet. This was the time to make a run for the door. This was the time to call 911. I couldn't move. I couldn't take my eyes off whoever or whatever was hunched up against the window.

"Say, listen," a voice muttered. "Who locked the screen?"

It had a voice, but it was still a shape.

Now I was by the window, the screen wire pushing in by a cheek plastered against it. My room was every kind of dark, and so was the night outside. The shape was darkest of all, but I saw all this tangled hair. A girl out there was trying to get in the window before she rolled off the porch roof.

It was a girl, so I wasn't so scared. Girls confused me, but they didn't scare me.

"Get back," I whispered, "so I can push the screen open."

The cheek pulled away. You could tell she was surprised to hear me. She was on all fours, swaying, edging back down the slant of the roof. The latch was tight, but I worked it loose. When I eased the screen open, it bumped her chin.

"Ouch," she said. "Watch it."

Then she sort of spilled into my room. She came in headfirst with all this flying hair. I thought she'd hit the floor first, but she did a little somersault. There she was at my feet. She seemed to be high-school size. I couldn't see her face, but she was looking up at me. That's when I remembered I was in my underwear.

"What do you think you're doing here?" she said in a whisper.

Shouldn't I be the one asking that?

"Never mind," she said. "I'm zonked."

She smelled funny. I definitely smelled alcohol. Now she was curled up right at my feet. "Forget about it," she said. And right away she was breathing steady with a little snore. She was sound asleep, dead to the world.

I wondered what she looked like and thought about turning on the light. I thought about going downstairs to tell Mom. Like, *Wake up, Mom. A girl fell in my window.*

Instead, I sat down on my bed to watch this shape tucked in under the windowsill with her knees drawn up to her chin. She seemed to be wearing a very short skirt and maybe boots. I decided to keep an eye on her till morning.

When I woke up, I was stretched out in bed, and sun was coming in green and gold through the vine leaves. For a minute I didn't remember. Then I looked for her, and she was gone. The screen was loose, unlatched. By noon I almost decided I'd dreamed her.

But when night came again, I latched the screen.

It must have been midnight when I heard her boot skid on the drainpipe. I was awake again and waiting, not so worried this time. I even grinned in the dark, thinking about her with one boot on the trellis and the other trying to wedge onto the drainpipe, heaving herself up, trying to get back in without waking the whole neighborhood.

Her knees thumped on the porch roof. The room went darker when she loomed up at the window. Now she was slipping long nails under the screen. Now she was figuring out it was latched again.

I slid out of bed and crept to the sill. "You again," I said.

"You again," she said. "Let me in. Make it snappy." Her voice was blurry, and we were nose-to-nose with screen wire between. Her breath smelled like a brewery.

This time she threw a leg over the sill and stepped into the room. To steady herself, she grabbed my wrist. There were splotchy spots on her hands. They were all sticky. Her bracelets jangled, and her sweater had a smoky smell. She ran a messy hand through her hair, but it fell back to shadow her face. She seemed to stare around the room and then at me.

"What's the big idea?" she said, weaving.

"Are you sneaking back in?" I whispered. "Like after a date?"

"Ssh." She put a finger to her lips. "You'll wake my mom."

"It's not your mom," I said. "It's my mom. You're crawling into the wrong house. You've had too much to drink."

"Drink?" she said. "Just make it a small one for me, and then I'll have to go." But she was going already. Her knees buckled, and she slid down the wall, asleep before she hit the floor.

This is ridiculous, I thought. But the next thing I knew, it was morning, and she was gone again.

Mom didn't know if she wanted me in the house or out of it while she was at work. That morning I walked the entire town. There were no shadows during the day. It was just this boring town simmering in the sun. I even walked up and down the rows of trucks in the I.G.A. parking lot. I walked all four sides of the park, with the water tower in the center of it and not even a wading pool for little kids. I had lunch at Grandma's and walked the whole town again in the afternoon. Tonight I wanted to be really tired.

Of course I might have dreamed her. The girl. I might have dreamed her up because I didn't know anybody else. But in dreams you hardly ever smell people's breath.

That night I latched the screen as usual and left a light on. Anybody crawling up on the roof could see in and know it wasn't her room, right? It made sense to me. I went to sleep by the light of the lamp on the dresser.

Any little sound outside would have sent me rocketing out of the bed, but it was a quiet night. I only woke up because the lamp made me think it was morning. Somebody was standing at the dresser. By the light of the little lamp, she was combing out her long tangled hair. She was all dressed up and ready to rumble. I couldn't see her face in the foggy mirror. She could. She was looking herself over. Then she turned and looked at me.

"If I can't get rid of you," she said, quiet but clear, "I might as well take you with me. You might come in handy."

"Where?" I whispered.

"Where can you go in a town like this? Just out. Come on."

When my feet hit the floor, boards creaked. "Shh," she said. "Remember Mom."

I just stood there.

"You want to put on some clothes?" she said.

So this was happening. In dreams you often aren't wearing *anything*. When I'd pulled on shorts and a shirt, I turned to the door.

"Not that way." She jerked a thumb at the window. "You have a lot to learn."

Then we were both outside, crawling down the slant of the roof, ladies first. She'd had practice swinging herself over the gutter and shinnying down the drainpipe. I followed, scraping a knee on the tin. I wanted to climb down the trumpet vine, but it wasn't there. Trumpet vines don't just crawl away. But I was more worried about getting dizzy. I don't like heights. I dangled, and dropped.

We went around the house and started along the street. "Where are we going?" I said because we were going somewhere. We weren't just strolling.

"What you don't know, you can't blab," she said. "But think about it. Summer's over, and school's about to start—senior year. You know how senior year starts around here. Everybody knows that."

I didn't.

Now we were coming up on the park. A line of cars were pulled up at the curb, all classics. A few low-riders, a customized '57 Chevy. Under the park trees people were sitting at picnic tables. High-school people—seniors with sideburns. Girls with long falls of hair. People with beers and boots. They looked straight through me, but it was pretty exciting.

What they said I couldn't follow. High school talks its own language. And they kept their voices down. "Who brought the paint?" somebody said, and I heard that.

Somebody lifted a box out of the weeds and handed around cans of spray paint. "Far out," somebody said.

They were drifting now, like shadows, to the long metal legs of the town water tower. From down here it looked a mile high, with a winking red light on top to warn planes. I sort of knew then what was happening.

They started up a metal ladder. Their cleats rang as they

climbed like a long centipede senior. The girl hung back, then hitched a boot on the lowest rung. "Stay close behind me," she said over her shoulder. "Catch me if I fall."

She was a tough girl, but scared now. She didn't like climbing any higher than a porch roof. I didn't either, but I was more scared of being left behind, down in the shadowy park. I didn't want to be left out while the seniors spray-painted their year across the big round tank like a spaceship above us. Either way I was scared, so I went up.

Above the trees it was cooler. I looked up to keep from looking down. The first seniors were already up there, working their way around a rickety catwalk. The girl and I got higher and higher till we were there too. I forgot and looked down at streetlights winking through trees and out to dark fields and more fields.

They went to work with the cans hissing in their hands, spraying the giant letters coiling around the tank: CLASS OF—

They wanted letters taller than they could reach. They bounced on the catwalk to get higher, and metal moved under our feet. I hugged the water tank, and I really didn't feel so good.

Now they thought of how to do it. Before she could say anything, two guys lifted up the girl. She held a spray can, and her hands were splotchy with paint. She caught her breath but wouldn't show how scared she was. She worked as high as she could reach, up there on the guys' shoulders, spraying in the giant, looping letters so the whole town could see that the seniors had left their mark. Fresh paint glistened in the dim light.

Time skipped a beat. I saw when her hand with the spray can swayed away from the tank. The catwalk rattled. The guys grabbed for her. But she'd lost her balance.

She collapsed into the air, off their shoulders, out of their hands. Her arms flew out, and the spray can fell faster than she did, end over end into the night. She screamed all the way down to sudden silence, and the dark went darker.

She'd told me to catch her, but I couldn't. How could I? Every second she fell was a year, and I couldn't do anything. All I could do was scream my head off, up there on the tower above the town, and finally I was all alone.

You probably saw it in the paper. I was headline news and made my name in this town before anyone knew what it was:

SLEEPWALKING BOY
RESCUED FROM WATER TOWER

VOLUNTEER FIRE DEPARTMENT
CALLED OUT IN MIDDLE OF NIGHT TO
TALK DOWN FRIGHTENED YOUTH

INCIDENT RECALLS 30-YEAR-OLD
TRAGEDY WHEN SENIOR GIRL FELL
FROM TOWER IN SPRAY-PAINT PRANK

So she hadn't been a dream, but she wasn't real either. She'd died in a fall from the water tower all those years ago. My room up in the attic at the back of the house had been her room then. She'd gone out that window and across that back porch roof on a late-summer night just before school started.

Now, all these years later on late-summer nights, she wants back in.

The Most Important Night of Melanie's Life

When Melanie suspected she'd have to baby-sit her brothers, she made a plan to be over at April's house. She and April were best buds. Melanie had listened on the extension to hear her mother talking about the party she and Dad would be going to. It was a business thing, wives included. So Melanie was ready when her mother mentioned it.

"Absolutely not. I have to be at April's. It's only the most important night of my life."

"What's happening at April's?" her mother asked.

Nothing was planned. April hadn't even sounded that happy about Melanie coming over, so Melanie said, "Mother, if you keep prying into my private life, I may have to go on drugs or something. Do I have to account to you for every minute? I'm fourteen."

So her mother offered her the going baby-sitter rate with ten dollars on top to sweeten the deal.

Melanie turned her down flat. "It's a matter of principle. If I start baby-sitting the boys, you and Dad will be going out every month or so. I won't be a teenager. I'll be your slave. The twins are only nine, and the baby's seven. They're going to need sitting for years. I'll be an old woman by then."

Melanie knew she'd won when her mother sighed, "I sure miss Trish." Up till last summer they could count on Trish from next door, but now she was away at college. "I guess we'll have to find somebody else."

"Do that," Melanie said.

Then the boys put up an argument. "Hey, we don't need a sitter," the twins, Mike and Mark, said. "Give us the money and we'll sit Clem." Clem, the seven-year-old, said nothing, but looked pained that anybody thought he needed any supervision. "We're way too old for a baby-sitter," Mike and Mark said. "Add our ages together, and we're eighteen."

Then they found out the baby-sitter was a guy. They didn't know him. His name was Ben, a nephew of the Hutchinsons', three streets over, visiting.

"What kind of guy baby-sits?" Melanie rolled her eyes.

"One who likes kids," a twin said.

"And money," the other one said.

Then they heard he was sixteen. "Wow," the twins said. "He'll be in high school."

"Cool," Clem said softly.

It was rain turning to sleet that night, and Ben was late. Dad stood in the front hall, jingling his car keys. "We ought to be there now," he said, "and the streets are glazing over." Mom was all dressed up and ready too. Melanie came down the stairs in a stocking cap and her down jacket from Urban Outfitters.

"Honey, we've got to leave," her mother said. "Just hang around till Ben gets here."

Melanie smacked her own forehead. "You've got to be kidding. What if he doesn't show? Then I'm stuck here all evening with these dweebs. No way."

She was out the door, aiming at April's. Dad's keys were jangling like church bells. So finally Mike and Mark promised they wouldn't even move till the sitter got there.

When their parents were gone, silence fell over the house.

"It's like *Home Alone,*" Mike said in a spooky voice.

"It's neat," Mark said.

Before they could work up a plan, they heard a sound outside. Feet scraping on the welcome mat. When they opened the front door, Ben was there, filling it up. He was definitely high school. He wore a flight jacket, black jeans, ball cap on backward. Ice crystals gleamed in his sideburns, and his eyes seemed to see farther than a kid's.

"Wow, you sure are tall," Mike said. "How tall are you?"

They crowded around him but let him in. He was wearing big boots.

"You probably drive," Mark said. "Did you drive over here?"

In those first moments Ben's mind seemed far away. "No, I walked," he said, "partway."

"We're Mike and Mark," the twins said. "You can't tell us apart. This is Clem. He's the baby. He's only seven."

Then Ben did a fantastic thing. He reached down and shook hands with all of them, even Clem. So it wasn't like having a baby-sitter at all. Ben's hands were ice cold, but at sixteen you probably don't even have to wear gloves.

In the living room he towered over them, gazing around almost like he was surprised to be here. "We could run some movies," Mike said. "You ever see *Nightmare on Elm Street?*"

Ben looked down at them. "I've seen something scarier than that."

"What?" Clem said, hugging himself.

"You guys!" Ben said, and they all yelled and started punching one another because Ben was great.

They didn't even turn on the TV. They got out their baseball cards to show. Clem brought out the plastic dinosaur skeleton he'd put together from a kit. They had hot chocolate and a big bag of pretzels. Ben hadn't taken off his flight jacket. He said he couldn't seem to warm up, so they decided to have a fire in the fireplace. He showed them how to lay it and let Clem light it.

They were all hunkered down on the hearth, so now it was like a campfire. Mike said, "You know any stories? They got to be scary." Ben thought about that, rubbing his chin. He shaved.

"All my stories are too scary for you guys," he said, so they all yelled and pounded on one another until Ben began, "It was a dark and stormy night."

"Heard it," Clem said.

But they got him quieted down, and Ben told a story about a ghost in a tower somewhere in England. In life, the ghost had been a knight, so in stormy weather you could hear his armor rattle.

Clem's eyes got round.

A beautiful young girl came to visit this castle, and she started having these nightmares about a suit of armor. It was empty armor standing over in a corner. But in the dream she'd seen the finger on one of the chain-mail gloves move. Her nightmare drew her nearer and nearer. Something urged her to release whoever was inside.

Her dream hand came out to lift the helmet's visor. There within, staring back at her, were the empty eye sockets of an ancient skull. Black beetles glittered in the sockets, but all other life had long fled. Her screams echoed down all the corridors you get in nightmares.

The twins and Clem were sitting closer to Ben now.

The dream returned until the girl was no longer able to sleep. One night she threw back the bedcovers. Wide awake, she was drawn up the turning steps, higher and higher into the tower. Holding a flickering candle aloft, she came upon a heavy door that swung open. In the corner stood the suit of ar mor she'd known from a dozen nightmare nights. She moved nearer. Her hand reached out. Hoping against hope that seeing the skull would rid her of her terrible dreams, she lifted the visor.

Inside the helmet a young man's piercing eyes met her gaze, but his voice was hollowed by the years. "I died too young, before I could love," he said. "Will you redeem me? Come away to share my lonely exile in a world beyond this one."

Ben's voice died out, and the crackling fire burned low. Clem's eyes were perfect circles. It was an okay story until the end.

"Ben, you know any stories without girls in them?" Mike asked.

Then behind them, the front door banged open. Feet stamped out in the hall. The twins and Clem jumped a foot.

Melanie stalked into the living room, jerking at her stocking cap and unzipping her down jacket. "Me and April had a major fight. She's such a—"

Ben was climbing to his feet, turning toward her. Melanie froze. "Oh, wow," she said, looking all the way up at him.

"I'm Ben." He put out a big hand.

The stocking cap fell from Melanie's grasp.

"Hey, Melanie, clear out," Mike said. "We're telling stories. No girls allowed."

"We've been having a great time," Ben said, just to her.

"Yeah," she said in a voice nobody had ever heard from her. "They're nice little boys."

She and Ben were shaking hands, very slow.

"You're in high school?" Melanie said in this new voice of hers. She seemed to be a bug caught in the beam of Ben's gaze.

"I was," he said.

"Better yet," Melanie murmured.

"You want to go out for a little while?" Ben asked her.

"Hey, no fair," Mark said.

"Why not?" Melanie said. "Before my parents get back." Then in her regular voice she said to the twins and Clem, "You creeps don't even think about getting into trouble, okay? Like make my day, right?"

Ben reached down, swept up Melanie's stocking cap, and handed it back to her. They turned, very near each other, and walked out of the house without a backward glance.

Silence fell. Mike said, "I knew when he put that girl into the story, things were going to turn out stupid."

The three of them sat slumped before the dying embers of the fire. "What could he see in Melanie?" Mark wondered.

"It's a mystery," Clem said.

They forgot how long they sat there, watching the fire flicker out. Then they heard the sound of a car, and right away the front door banged open again. Their mother and then their dad raced into the living room, coats flapping. They didn't wipe their feet or anything. Their mother dropped to her knees and tried to get her arms around all three of them.

"Are you all right?" she gasped, trying to pull Clem closer. "What have you been doing all this time? We just got word from the Hutchinsons."

"Who are they?" Mike asked.

"Ben's aunt and uncle. Oh, it's too terrible. Ben . . . I shouldn't even tell you."

Their mother's hand covered her mouth. "Boys," Dad said, "the reason that Ben didn't come to sit for you tonight is that he had an accident. On his way here, he was struck by a hit-and-run driver. They found his body by the side of the road. He was dead before your mother and I ever left home tonight."

Now the eyes of all three of them, Mike and Mark and Clem, were perfect circles.

"And where's Melanie?" their mother asked, looking around. "Isn't she home yet?"

Waiting for Sebastian

Oh how I love the evening. Long summer evenings when the shadows of the trees creep in silent shapes across the lawn until they merge with night. I watch from this high window, framed by the old curtains held back by silk cords. I toy with the cords and watch the world dim.

When I was very small, too small to climb up on this windowseat, I didn't like being put to bed when the window was still bright with summer light. I fought sleep and woke again to velvet dusk, hearing the sounds of the house beneath my cot. Only a cot then for my infant self—not like the proper grown-up bed in the room now.

The whole house and I listened to the parties Mama and Papa gave, the crystal sounds of the dinner table floating up the flights. The bark of the men's laughter and the rising scent of their cigars after the silken sound of the ladies retiring. I love summer evenings because they take their time, dangling the dark before you.

But winter evenings warm my heart. I don't feel the cold. I watch from this window as the sun drops like a blazing penny through the bare branches, and darkness comes like a surprise.

It's winter now, the shortest day, and the sun is hurrying into the earth. This is the evening I wait for all through the year. I am curled in the windowseat at the top of the house with the cat alert in my lap. This cat is a tortoiseshell, up from the barn and quite wild, but she likes me. She gazes up, perplexed and admiring. Nanny used to say that I too had been born in a barn, when I was smaller and naughtier. "Born in a barn," when I forgot to close the door behind me or grew tiresome in the bath.

From here the cat and I can see right to the end of the drive now the leaves have fallen. Even the house around us waits. The statues in the lawn turn all their strange faces to the distant point where the drive meets the road. We all wait, breathless. Nothing trembles but my heart.

We get very little snow here, but in winter we are apt to get gales. They whip off the sea and cry in the attics and bend the trees double. This old window clatters in its frame, and the curtains billow, and the cord coils. Then the next morning the sky is scoured clean, and the gardener—Abel or whatever he is called—is out dragging the branches and lifting the twigs.

But this evening is still as a painting. This is the evening when my brother will be brought up from the station, home from school. The world waits for the car to turn in at the foot of the drive.

My brother Sebastian is coming home for his Christmas holidays, and I won't breathe or smile till he is here and this house is ringing with him. My brother Sebbie is coming home. But no. Wait. He says that Sebbie is a nursery name, and now that he is at school it would be a great crime if any of his friends knew. He is Sebastian now, and even Mama must call him by that name, when she remembers. My name is Charlotte, and I think I will keep it.

When my brother first went away to school, they thought I was too young to mind. How wrong they were, how very wrong. This house is always as empty as my heart when Sebastian isn't here, though it is full of people coming and going. Sebastian went away to school at seven. Boys do.

As Papa says, "Nothing good happens at home to a boy past the age of seven." Of course he is right. At seven boys need to live with one another in large, drafty brick places where they learn Latin verbs and tell one another terrifying tales. They eat cold cabbage and mashed potato with the eyes left in. And they are beaten when they are bad, which teaches them to be careful.

There are schools for girls to go away to, but Papa wouldn't hear of it. They play field hockey at such places, and it ruins their complexions and thickens their ankles. Papa says so. In the village there is a school where boys and girls go together, but Mama put her foot down. "When you are married, Charlotte, you will see quite enough of the opposite sex," Mama said. "I have."

So I learn at home. After Nanny retired to a cottage, a lady came to teach me German. She wore ribbed stockings and liked country walks, but she grew homesick for her Alpine valley. The vast front of her frock was awash with her tears, and she went away (Auf Wiedersehen, Fräulein).

After her, a lady came to teach me French. She was very pretty, and the scent of a rose garden followed where she went. She had vivid red lips, though she didn't paint them. Governesses mustn't. Because Nanny was gone by then, I forgot to close the door behind me. I saw Papa kissing the French governess. She didn't mind, so I wasn't worried, but I knew it was a secret. And so I told nobody but Mama. Soon after, on the very next day, that governess left too (Au revoir, mademoiselle).

Now I am quite on my own. But wait. Are those the headlamps of a car just turning up the drive? My forehead would be freezing, pressed against this frosty pane, if I felt the cold. Yes, the car that brings people from the station is coming up the drive. And I smile—too soon, but I can't help myself. The car takes forever, but now it's turning in the circle of gravel before the house. I peer down over the cat's ears to see—

But no. I know already it isn't Sebastian because he always bursts out of the back door before the car rolls to a stop. Sebastian with his necktie jerked round under his ear and his scarf in the school colors flying and his socks collapsing over his shoe tops . . .

Unless, of course, it is Sebastian—later. I turn away, hoping not to see him climb manlike out of the car, unfolding his great legs and planting his snub-nosed boots on the ground. Sebastian grown and firm-chinned under his braided cap, reaching back into the car for his kit. This is not the Sebastian I long for through the long year.

I make myself look, and it is neither of the Sebastians, nor anyone like them. It's other people, the nameless sort who come to stay and then go away. You can tell by their odd clothes and odd ways that they are foreign. Not proper visitors at all, and I can't think why Papa allows them. Perhaps we are poor now, and they pay to come here. I've thought of that. I've thought we might be poor and Mama and Papa don't want me to know—a secret to keep me from worrying. After all, what would a family be without secrets? We would be like strangers meeting in the train, telling one another everything about ourselves.

Yes, I suppose we must be poor now. I can't think when I last saw Mama ride, and I believe she has given up her horse. From this window I used to watch her descend the steps in her riding clothes, snapping the crop against her gathered skirts, stepping into the groom's hand to swing herself onto her hunter. And Papa doesn't shoot now. I have not heard the woods explode in gunfire or seen the birds rise in a panic for ages.

The driver comes round to lift the strangers' luggage down. A great mound of it rises on the gravel. I watch, and so does the cat, its ears like two tiny pyramids, motionless in an ancient Egyptian night. Two people, a man and a woman, climb out of the car. They are dressed any old way, with things on straps slung round their necks. My hand reaches for the silk cord as I watch them stalk up the steps as if they had every right.

Then, worse, someone steps out of the front door to greet them. Some perfect stranger welcomes them into our house.

Still, I am at my post like a sentry standing guard, though we have already been invaded. I don't know how long I cradle the uncomplaining cat, who thrusts out a paw and kneads my knee with its bunched claws. It might have been moments or hours we sat there. Time means nothing to me when Sebastian is not here.

Then the door of my nursery bursts open with a sound that stings me like a slap. I make quite certain to keep my door shut, now I am older. But it is banged back now, and the driver staggers in under the load of luggage from the car. I shrink behind the curtain, and the cat stands, arching its back, thinking of flight.

Like a dream one can't stop having, the strangers enter my room, the two from the car and the other who let them into our house. Here behind the curtain I can't see them and don't want to, though the room is flooded with sudden light.

"Why, what in the world!" someone says. "Some kind of kid's room?" She is foreign but not blind. She can see the dollhouse Papa gave me, and the rocking horse painted in the colors of Mama's hunter.

"That's right," says another voice, just as common but local. "This was Miss Charlotte's room."

Was and is.

"It's precious!" the foreign voice proclaims. "Isn't it precious? This stuff should all be in a museum, most of it. Shouldn't it?"

But her husband says nothing. He is still gasping from the climb. Six flights to reach my room up here beneath the roof, six flights with a turning at the top.

"And of course it was Mr. Sebastian's too, when they were both in the nursery. They had a nanny, nursery maids, governesses. Oh, you can't imagine the way people lived back then."

"No," the foreign woman murmurs. She is scanning the clutter of my room now. My dolls, propped in corners, gaze with their unblinking buttons at these intruders. The bear I loved to baldness fixes the invaders with his single eye. "But I don't know if—"

"Well, you see, as a rule we don't let this room. But just at the moment, we're expecting quite a large party. Perhaps in a day or so we can find you something on a lower floor."

I am always shy at the first sight of strangers. I edge back and the curtain moves, and they may have seen, so I brush the cat off my lap. It leaps down, below the hem of the curtain, and streaks in the direction of the door.

The foreign woman shrieks.

"Oh, I can't think how that cat got in," she is told. "I opened the window to air the room at midday. Perhaps it climbed the ivy on the walls. Cats do, pesky creatures."

She can't wait to leave the strangers in possession of my room, hoping they will settle. She shows them the device beside the bed that will make their tea, and she opens the cupboard where more blankets are. Then she is gone.

I listen, still as the statues, whilst the strangers make themselves at home, complaining of the cold, remarking on every lump in the bed. "It's not what I had in mind," the foreign woman says, but I hear them opening their valises, and I listen whilst they wander up and down the hall outside in search of the bathroom. The car has gone, and night has fallen. They won't stir themselves short of morning. They take a great liberty, it seems to me, but I suppose I must put up with them.

But no. They have confused me, and I had almost forgotten that this is the longest night, the night when Sebastian is expected and never comes. Now I must remember again what this night means, and what I must do.

At last the bed wheezes beneath the intruders. Then he must rise again and cross the room on freezing feet to turn off the light.

"I don't think I can figure out how that tea thing works," the woman says in the dark. But then they doze. He does. I can hear him, but it is fitful sleep in a strange bed in a place that does not want them.

The moon appears from behind a scudding cloud, and that suits me well enough. White light plays through the branches of the trees, and moonbeams shatter in the frost on the windowpane. Bright as day, as the saying goes. Now I must remember the meaning of this night, and who I am, and what I must do.

For this is the night we learned that we would not see Sebastian again. Oh, I don't mean he didn't come home. Nothing could have kept him away. They brought him home, and he is sleeping now, in the churchyard. Cold there, of course, but he feels it no more than I do. Oh yes, Sebastian came home, but not to me, who lived for his look, who died to be near him.

They did not notice how I grieved. Mama rode out, over the hedgerows and through the woods, letting the branches whip her face. She rode like a madwoman who hopes never to heal. Papa shut himself up in his study to pore over the maps of the place where Sebastian fell, as if the maps might be redrawn.

And I was all alone up here, wedged in the windowseat, watching for a car in the drive. Until on the longest night of the year I saw the answer plain before my face. The cord that held the curtains.

I looped it over the stout pole from which the curtains hung and wound it round my neck, fixing it tight. Then all I need do was spill myself like the cat, off the high windowseat. There was nothing to it. It was only the work of a moment, then forgotten a moment later. Naturally I could not know that it condemned me to this place forever. That I would remember once again each year on the longest night what I had done, and what I must repeat.

The cord is looped over the pole. Now I recall how often I have done it before. Oh, more than eighty times, I should think. With only a little surprise I feel the silken cord that never frays tighten around my neck. I imagine me outlined against the glaring moon. Once I have slipped off the window-seat, I will swing, head drooped against the frosty night.

How dreadful to awaken in that night and see me there.

Shadows

From the very beginning I knew the place was haunted. I wasn't frightened. Far from it. Ghosts were the company I came to count on.

An infant will fear, of course. The newest newborn fears falling and loud sounds. But my room was at the top of a long flight of stairs, so I was used to heights. As for loud sounds, ghosts are quiet as . . . the tomb.

Better yet, there were no other little girls about me to scream and shriek and tell hair-raising tales. I was a solitary child. I might have been lonely without my haunts.

I loved the dark. You're never alone in the dark. Or if you are, you can't be sure. Before I was old enough to roam the house, they came to me in my room. Just before sleeping, I'd often watch the closet door open. I'd see the little oval knob turning, blinking in the moonlight. Then hands—I don't know whose—would sort through my baby clothes. I'd drift toward sleep to the faint metallic music of the hangers scraping along the rod.

When I was no more than a toddler, things—beings— would pass me in the hall. I must have thought that even in these modern times there were women who still hid their faces in deep bonnets. And men, booted and spurred.

Only one of my spirits spoke, but that was later.

Every house on the river from here to Baton Rouge had haunts. It was expected, and the tourists liked it. More and more houses were open to the public, who were charged good money to be shown through. At Nottoway plantation they even served the public something called "brunch."

"Brunch," Aunt Sudie said, clamping her granite jaw. "Swilling vodka drinks on Sunday morning when they ought to be in church."

"Live and let live," sighed Aunt Margaret. Being sisters, they hardly ever agreed.

Our house was not open to the public. It was being kept in trust for me, for it seemed that I'd inherited it.

"Catch me opening this house to the public so a bunch of rednecks can tramp through and ruin the parquet!" said Aunt Sudie.

"Though heaven knows we could use the money," Aunt Margaret sighed.

"Margaret," Aunt Sudie said unfairly, "you're money crazy. Money is your middle name."

I was so young, I thought it really was.

Aunt Sudie and Aunt Margaret Money were spinsters in the best Southern tradition, except they were from New York. In a rare moment of agreement, they'd decided to be Southern. They napped and sipped sun tea through the heat of the day and read the New Orleans *Times-Picayune*. They took up the habit of funeral-parlor fans and sat sniping at Yankees.

I was said to be New York–born too, but I was being brought up as a Southern child. Even as a baby I wore a tiny heart-shaped locket, an heirloom that couldn't have come down through the family. And I was allowed to run barefoot well into winter.

Though I never minded the Louisiana heat, the aunts suffered with it. In New York, Aunt Sudie had been in charge of something called a typing pool, which had a cool, refreshing sound. Aunt Margaret had skied once, on real snow. Though it had tired her, she never tired of recalling it.

They worked hard at being eccentrics, but how could I know that? I'd met stranger beings than they on the nighttime stairs.

One of their oddities was that they were content to appear older than they were. When I first remember her, Aunt Margaret must still have been in her thirties, though she was fading fast. And Aunt Sudie was the sort who'd never really been young.

They let themselves go. Aunt Sudie, who gardened, wore her denim pants, rolled to the knee, even indoors. Aunt Margaret, who kept house in a vague way, wore housedresses that zipped up. They both went gray early and did nothing about it.

They weren't real aunts. They'd been friends of my parents, who were said to be dead. By all accounts my father really was dead. But my mother, always spoken of sadly in past tense, occasionally wrote to the aunts. Her envelopes were powder blue, and the stamps were sometimes foreign.

With a child's wisdom, I thought a mother who had no time for me wasn't worth missing. And I wouldn't have fretted over the death of a parent. The creatures of my nights upstairs had erased the border between the living and the dead.

Though the neighbors never came near us, we weren't alone. There was a little house, a dependency, standing out in the cedar swamp behind us. The farmland had been sold off long since to the oil companies, and so this little cabin, steep-roofed in the Cajun way, stood just at the end of our world. Though I wasn't to go near it, I knew people lived in that house. A very old woman sometimes came out to sweep the bald yard and throw feed at the chickens who lived under the floor.

Never very maternal, the aunts rarely tucked me in. I spent many a night with chin propped on the windowsill, watching the flickering glow from the cabin as figures inside moved in yellow lamplight. Sometimes I slept the night through at the window, waking in that quiet moment of dawn after the dead slept and the living hadn't stirred.

I was five when my special spirit came to me the first time. By then I was ready for the change of going to school. I'd already explored all the world allotted to me. I'd climbed the forbidden levee and all the trees I could manage. I'd swung upside down from low branches while my skirt settled around my face. I'd taunted dead snakes in the river road with long sticks. I'd even grown a little weary of my ghosts, who were as restless as I.

Then one night, moonlit of course, there was a new shadow in the room. I was used to grown-up ghosts: gaunt women who wept wordlessly, gray military men who stared sadly at their empty sleeves. But this new shadow, dark against the moon-white wall, was hardly taller than I.

I looked for petticoats. Dead daughters were often beautifully dressed for burial. But I saw only the hint of bare feet. I looked for a deep bonnet, as my shadows never liked showing their faces. But moonlight played on pale flesh. The eyes were deep-set and dark. I was interested at once. It seemed to be a boy.

He was watching me, but then they all did. He moved along the wall. Had he entered from the door or the closet? I hadn't noticed.

I thought he would fade. They often did. I watched him drift. When he crossed before the closet door, he was lost in the darkness of walnut wood. But he moved on through a final glare of moonlight to the darkest corner. There he lingered, looking at me. I drew up on my elbows, wondering if his eyes would glow. Eyes in that corner often did.

I looked until I saw him better. No staring revealed his eyes, but I made out the small circle of his mouth. Then I heard the ghost of a sound. It seemed to be his bare toes curling on the floorboards. It might just as well have been some small creature in the walls. We had plenty of them too.

I tried something new, something not done. "Who goes there?" I said, almost aloud.

I expected no answer and got none, though the room was full of his listening. I knew he heard, so I slept, satisfied.

He came again and again. Not every night, but often. Once I was just drifting off when the rag rug beside my bed came alive and moved. He was edging out from under my bed, turning his shadowed face up to see if I saw. The mop of his hair was paler than his face. I could have reached down and touched him, but I thought better of it.

Another time he stepped forthrightly out of the closet as soon as I was in bed. At last I expected him there. I even imagined he guarded me while I slept, though there was nothing to be guarded against.

I went to school, but it was a disappointment. The children were all too . . . real. I couldn't fathom the rules of their games. They were forever dividing into teams to defeat each other. But at least I learned to read.

I even read storybooks in bed, but soon gave that up. The bright light kept my ghosts away, and so the room was too lonely. I left my lamp dark, and the boy returned. One night when he was a shadow in the corner, I sat up and said, "What was your name?"

The whole room caught its breath. Then I heard some sort of answer, unless it was the breeze in the trees.

"Seth," he seemed to say.

"Seth? Seth what? Calhoun? Randolph? Deschamps?" I named all the oldest families in the local graveyard.

"Just Seth," said he or the breeze.

On another night he seemed to settle. He sat in his corner cross-legged in a flowing, old-fashioned shirt. It looked hand-me-down and gravely dingy. His trousers rode up his white legs. Dressed no better for burial than this, he must have been a poor boy.

Too poor to be schooled, perhaps.

"Seth," I said, "do you know your letters? The alphabet?"

He and the room thought about that.

"Teach me," I heard from somewhere.

Proud of my own knowledge, I plumped up my pillow and began, soft for fear I'd frighten him into fading. "A for apple."

I heard an echo.

"B for boy."

I heard it again.

Through nights, seasons, semesters, we worked at the alphabet and simple spelling. When I came to third grade and the multiplication tables, I passed them along to the shadow in the corner. If I was too sleepy for our lesson, I heard in my dreams a distant voice prompting me: "Seven eights are fifty-six."

In fourth grade we did geography at school. At night I taught world capitals, sketching the shapes of countries in the night air while eyes watched from the corner. "Caracas, Venezuela," I'd say.

"LaPaz, Bolivia," the corner answered.

A child dreads changes, but they come. I was a while noticing that as I grew, so too did Seth. I got longer in the leg, lanky as a colt. By moonlight I saw Seth's hands resting on his knees. His hands were wider, the knees bigger. When he loomed into the room, he threw the shadow of a man. I hadn't known that ghosts grow, but I never looked for logic in the dark.

In the summer after sixth grade, I got a licking I didn't deserve. In a burst of housecleaning, Aunt Margaret took a feather duster to my room and found bits of burned tobacco in the corner.

She reported at once to Aunt Sudie. Lurking, I heard. "Quite apart from anything else," Aunt Margaret sighed, "she could burn the house down around our ears."

Aunt Sudie said less and went for the yardstick.

She walloped me, and I wept at the injustice of it. They sent me to my room, a meaningless place during the day. I sat huddled on the stairs, hearing them.

"She is getting to the difficult age," Aunt Margaret sighed. "Now our troubles begin."

"Girls!" Aunt Sudie said, immensely disgusted.

I sulked, but I was secretly pleased. The ghost, Seth, had reached the age when boys sneak smokes. But he hadn't smoked in my presence. He was too old-fashioned and courtly for that. He'd smoked only when I slept. Treated like a lady, I heard the first promise of womanhood.

Seventh grade was too much for me, and I gave in to it. At school I joined the other girls at the washroom mirror. We stared at ourselves, hoping our faces would clear and our busts appear. We dreamed of leading cheers and being loved. I began to notice living boys.

But I didn't like them much. They were loud and never alone. They moved in a pack and would not be taught, even by teachers. How could I say to some basketball-dribbling boy, "Caracas, Venezuela," and expect the proper reply?

Yet the living boys, the daylight boys, drove my Seth away. He went as quietly as he'd come. Or perhaps I stopped looking for him and so he wasn't there.

The light burned in my bedroom till all hours. I had a little radio now, beside my bed, blaring hard rock while I experimented with color on my fingernails. I read beauty tips in magazines suspended by my drying fingers. My nights were as bright as my days.

Then it was senior year, and I was all but grown. The aunts flooded the house with the catalogues of distant colleges, hoping I'd go far away so they could have my house to themselves.

I was willing to go. I'd have left that house, that life, without a backward thought, except Seth came back.

On that last night, I'd packed my college clothes and dropped into bed, but it was too sultry for sleep. I found myself at the window, gazing into the heavy night. Though I'd long ago ceased wondering about the cabin among the cedars, I saw it now. Faint yellow light fell in a square from its open door. I'd never seen that door open at night, or perhaps I'd forgotten.

When I turned back to bed, I knew I wasn't alone. Beside my piled suitcases was the shadow of a man. His outline was between me and the door. Looking for some refuge, I reached far back and found a name. "Seth?" I said, hoping it was he.

His mop of hair was pale in the black room. He worked his big hands together. In a voice deep but soft, he spoke. "I couldn't rest easy without saying good-bye."

I'd forgotten what my childhood had taught me, so I was frightened. I went cold, and my teeth chattered when I said, "You knew I was going away."

He nodded, perhaps smiled. "We're both going away, but to different places."

He looked down at himself, and I saw he'd outgrown the flowing shirt. He wore something dark with bright buttons blinking in the gloom. "I've joined the army," he said.

His uniform should be gray, I thought, Confederate gray. But it wasn't.

"If it hadn't been for you," he said, "I wouldn't have been schooled at all. I'd only have known the swamps and the bayous. But for you, there'd have been no one to learn from, or love."

He turned to go. I heard his boots on the floor, stealthy but real. "Much obliged," he said.

He was at the door now, ready to walk down through the silent house and back to the cedar swamp.

I knew everything then, almost.

"Seth?" I said, too loud.

He stopped, too sudden for a ghost, and turned humanly back.

"Whose son are you, Aunt Sudie's or Aunt Margaret's?"

A light glowing down the hall caught the profile of the living man.

"It don't matter," he said, and smiling, he left me.

The Present

"This place where you live, this Indiana,"
he said to change the subject. "How big a city is it?"
—"The Kiss in the Carry-on Bag"

"Shadows" is a story in which the ghosts turned out to be only background figures, window dressing. They fall away at the end to reveal two characters, a living girl and boy on the threshold of adulthood, about to walk into the world.

That story speaks of the "quiet moment of dawn after the dead slept and the living hadn't stirred." We emerge now from four stories that feature night at the windows into the full blaze of day to question life as it's lived here in the morning of a new, changeable century.

These next stories are a mixed bag of assorted epiphanies: a conniving cat and not one but two tough old ladies who have reached the century mark. And a pair of very different stories about how boy meets girl.

We even encounter yet another character named Sebastian, a name that last cropped up in the story called "Waiting for Sebastian." Is there a link between these two characters who share a name? No. It's just that I'd forgotten I'd used the name before. After more than thirty years of writing, you don't remember the names of all your characters. I can't. There are probably writers who could conduct computer searches and Google out all the names they'd used to be digitally stored. I'm not one of those people.

I'm not much given to talking animals either. The heroine of "Fluffy the Gangbuster" is one of a kind in my work. She speaks cat patois, though, and wouldn't lower herself to communicate with humans anyway. But a cat with a plan is, like ghosts, a picturesque way of telling a story about live humans. And this story explores an issue I've worked before: the contrast between gang membership and real friendship. It harks back to the first story in this collection. I'll say less about "The Kiss in the Carry-on Bag" because there's a surprise in the middle of it. But it was inspired by an actual historic celebration that I observed by standing in the crowds outside a European palace. You never know when a writer might be right there beside you, hunting and gathering for a future story.

Or as Gene says in the story "I Go Along," "It's weird, like there could be poets around and you wouldn't realize they were there." His story is the clearest example in this collection of the epiphany. In a moment he's been unconsciously moving toward, he suddenly sees he's been living the wrong life. This story also asks most directly the question:

WHEN WILL I START TAKING
CHARGE OF MY LIFE?

This present-tense grouping, and the collection, conclude with "The Three-Century Woman." It's my own favorite kind of story, one that hopes to erase distance between young and old, to narrow the generation gap. There's an elderly character in every one of my novels—for fear there aren't enough elders in the lives of my readers.

Great-grandma Breckenridge is my kind of old person, one with plenty of fight left in her. I created her by imagining what the title character of that short story "The Special Powers of Blossom Culp" might be like much, much later in life.

This last one is a story about storytelling, about how fiction is the vine that flourishes on the tree trunk of the real.

Fluffy the Gangbuster

Every day after school, they all made a beeline for Aunt Agnes's house.

Guthrie (a boy) seemed to leave school by the north door, but doubled back to a restroom with two entrances. He'd go in one and out the other and had his secret escape plan from there.

Blair (a girl), who was the quickest of them all, left school by the south door. She'd hunker down between two Saturns in the teachers' parking lot. Then make a break for it.

Wyatt (a boy) left school through an air duct he knew about in the heating plant. Being small, he could fit in anywhere, and he too was quick.

Roxie (a girl) wasn't. She'd leave by the front door in a crowd of people and saunter across Roosevelt Road with them. Then she'd merge with a snowball bush near that corner, and it was only a half block from there through alleys to Aunt Agnes's.

Each by a different route, they all turned up at her house daily unless somebody had a dental appointment.

"Anybody see us?" they'd ask when they were assembled on the porch. It was screened by spirea bushes and considered safe.

By "anybody," they meant Taylor Trumble and Taylor's gang, "Trumble's Troublemakers." As everybody knows, gangs are starting earlier these days. Taylor was big as a ninth grader and mean as a snake and had the Troublemakers organized as early as kindergarten. They'd been shaking people down for years. There was a rumor that they were packing boxcutters now, and nobody wanted to find out if it was true.

The Troublemakers went after everybody, but they were really out to get Guthrie, Blair, Wyatt, and Roxie because they were close friends. Taylor worried about people who hung out together just because they were friends and didn't even seem to have a leader to boss them. They all carried their lunch money in their socks, and Wyatt could show you a chipped tooth.

When they were sure they hadn't been followed, they'd troop through the screen door into the living room where the card table was set up and waiting. So was Fluffy. Fluffy was Aunt Agnes's indoor/outdoor cat, and Fluffy was a problem. As even Aunt Agnes said, "It's hard to make a good Christian out of a cat."

For a cat her size, she was an excellent jumper and spent nap time on top of the refrigerator in a turkey platter. But she always knew when the kids were due. She'd drift into the living room where the Monopoly board was set up. Leaping on the table, she'd scatter the Monopoly money, gnaw the corners of the board, shed on everything, make trouble. But when she heard the kids hit the porch, she'd vanish, though she never went far. If you checked out the room, you'd see a pair of wicked amber eyes trained on you from behind the piano. Or there'd be a lump in the curtains halfway up, and that would be Fluffy.

Aunt Agnes was like her house, which had a big front porch and was real old. She was the last cookie baker in any of their lives, and her kitchen smelled partly of fresh-baked brownies and partly of Fluffy. The Monopoly set had been Aunt Agnes's when she was a girl, so it was ancient. Because she was Guthrie's great-aunt, he was always the banker. He wore a green visor he'd seen in a movie about Las Vegas and shook the dice high above his head.

Miraculously, all the original tokens were still there. Guthrie always picked the little racing car. Blair went for the cannon. Wyatt chose the top hat, and Roxie took the purse. Partly thanks to Fluffy, none of the original Monopoly money had survived. It had been replaced by construction-paper counterfeit currency. Most of the Community Chest and Chance cards were still there, though chewed. Unfortunately, all thirty-two houses and twelve hotels were missing. Aunt Agnes said she hadn't seen them since the war, and she didn't say which war.

So she replaced them with a little dish of candies, the kind with chocolate on the inside that melts in your mouth, not in your hand. She'd count out thirty-two green candies for the houses and twelve red for the hotels. These the foursome used when they were buying real estate for their properties. They weren't for eating and were covered in cat hair, but they led to trouble every time.

Each afternoon was the same. Though they stretched the regulation rules and somebody was always coming up with a new one, they started the right way. Beginning with Guthrie, each player threw the dice, and the player with the highest total started the play. The only unbreakable rule was the Aunt Agnes Law, which stated that whoever was ahead at five-thirty was declared winner and everybody went home.

Wyatt was the historian of the group and knew all there was to know about the beginnings of Monopoly. "It's a little-known fact," he'd say, "that Charles B. Darrow of Germantown, Pennsylvania, the inventor of Monopoly, struck a deal with Parker Brothers in 1935 to produce twenty thousand Monopoly sets per week.

"Equally amazing, Monopoly has appeared in nineteen separate languages.

"It is also interesting to note that place names for the game all come from locations in Atlantic City, New Jersey."

"It's a well-known fact and *not* interesting to note," Roxie would say, "that you've already told us this a thousand times." Roxie had the shortest attention span in the group. It got shorter if she landed on Park Place when it was loaded with four chocolate houses and a chocolate hotel and cost her two thousand dollars.

"And bear in mind," Wyatt would point out, "we're talking Depression-era money, when two thousand dollars wasn't chicken feed or chump change."

And so it went, every afternoon from school till five-thirty. Everybody always understood when Roxie tried to palm a Go To Jail card back into the pile. Everybody was braced for Blair's piercing shriek when she drew the Community Chest card authorizing her to collect fifty dollars from each player. And everybody helped Banker Guthrie count out the money because he was only at grade level in his math skills. They were the four citizens of their private Monopoly board world, a tiny Atlantic City, fraying at the edges. They strolled its streets together, from Mediterranean Avenue to Boardwalk, rolling the dice as they went.

Roxie, who could get antsy, sometimes said, "This isn't a board game. It's a *bored* game," and she'd spell out the difference. But nobody ever wanted it to end.

"Let's still be playing this in high school," Blair would say. "Okay?"

And five-thirty always came too soon. They left Aunt Agnes's pretty much the way they left school. They knew Trumble's Troublemakers had found out where they were every afternoon. Taylor Trumble's spies were everywhere, and there was a beeper on Taylor's belt.

Usually by five-thirty the Troublemakers were working the mall, but you couldn't be too careful. Roxie left quietly over the front porch railing, dropping down behind the spirea bushes, then working her way left some days, right the others. Guthrie went out the back and then between two garages because he lived in that direction. Blair sometimes used the front door, sometimes the back, sprinted to the fence line between Aunt Agnes's property and the Clevelands' and followed it back to the alley. From there she went home at an angle through people's backyards.

Wyatt didn't trust doors. At five-thirty he'd excuse himself to go upstairs to the bathroom. Then he'd climb out the bathroom window, shinny down a drainpipe, and he was out of there. Though Aunt Agnes was aware of all this exiting, she just thought it was the sort of weird things kids do.

But they never broke up without an argument. The longer the game went on, the fewer green chocolate houses and red chocolate hotels there were. They seemed to melt away. By the end of the game, there were never more than twenty-eight of the houses and never more than nine hotels. They had to send out to the kitchen for more. "Who's eating the real estate?" Guthrie would say in his position as banker.

You couldn't blame Roxie or she'd throw a fit. When suspicion fell on Blair, she'd say, "I'm dieting. I didn't even have a brownie. Taylor Trumble took my lunch money today because I wasn't wearing socks, and I didn't even care." Wyatt was quick enough to eat all of Atlantic City before you knew it was gone, but he looked as innocent as a choirboy. Of course it could be Guthrie himself. Nobody knew.

"You can't blame Fluffy for this," he said. "Cats don't process chocolate. Ask a vet." Then five-thirty crept up on them, and they quit quibbling, declared a winner, returned the dish with the remaining chocolates to the kitchen, and made their ways home.

The living room fell silent after they left, with only the distant sound of Aunt Agnes out in the kitchen, banging pans. It was quiet time for Fluffy, who by then was on the windowsill, still as a sphinx.

There was much they didn't know about Fluffy, or in fact about any cat. Humans simply don't know that cats understand every word they hear spoken. After all, they've lived thousands of years with people, and there's nothing wrong with their hearing. Now, you take a dog. A dog understands simple words and commands and is all too willing to obey. But cats don't like to obey, so they act like you're talking gibberish. And don't think they can't recognize their names, because they can. But Fluffy didn't like hers. She'd have preferred something more Egyptian because she had ancestors who'd been worshiped in Egypt.

Fluffy wasn't your ordinary cat. If there was cat school, she'd be in the Gifted program. Of course she'd occasionally come out of hiding to climb around under the card table like any common cat, throwing her tail and butting ankles. It was a cat thing. And that business of messing up the Monopoly board before they got there was just to let them know whose turf they were on. But there was more to Fluffy than that.

She'd grown as fond of Guthrie, Blair, Wyatt, and Roxie as a cat can. She wasn't a real people-cat. She wasn't about to sit on your lap. But the daily Monopoly game gave her something to look forward to. She liked listening to the conversation, though they bickered and quibbled too much. She slept through some of it.

From the windowsill, or up on the curtain when she was sharpening her claws, Fluffy could watch the room with one amber eye and the yard with the other. It came to her attention that there was often another group of kids lurking outside, darting under bushes, moving from tree to tree, that sort of thing. They weren't there every day, but when they were, she knew.

They were the Troublemakers gang, of course, about whom she'd heard so much from the Monopoly players. And the big ugly one with the nose ring was Taylor Trumble, who was trouble indeed. Fluffy kept her eye on them. She knew that Trumble's Troublemakers were the enemy. And if there's one thing a cat understands, it's an enemy.

She knew Guthrie, Blair, Wyatt, and Roxie were scared to death of Trumble's Troublemakers. Cats can smell fear, and she smelled enough fear to make her amber eyes water. Fluffy supposed she was simply going to have to do something. It would take higher-level thinking, but Fluffy rather suspected herself of being a genius.

Over many days—weeks, really—Fluffy thought about the Cleveland family, who lived next door across the fence. Then she examined her claws. She hadn't done much digging lately. You can't call scratching around in the litter box real digging. Then she thought about the chocolate candies the kids used in place of houses and hotels for the Monopoly board. She thought long, and she thought hard. And Fluffy came up with a plan.

That's where the missing red and green chocolate candies went. Fluffy took them, a few at a time. There was plenty of opportunity. In the middle of the game the players all trooped out to the kitchen, where the Agnes person fed them cookies and milk. There was all the time in the world for Fluffy to spring off the windowsill, creep on little cat feet across the rug, soar like a gazelle onto the table, and step carefully across the board to the candy dish. With a small sandpaper tongue she'd scoop up a few candies and carry them away in her mouth. Often she had time to make several trips.

Her storehouse was behind the piano, a cool, dark place too narrow to dust. There in time a mound of candy grew. Once she found a bug back there, scuttling toward Candy Mountain on many legs. She ate it.

Guthrie had been right about one thing. Cats can't process chocolate. It's the sugar. Fluffy carried the candies in a dry mouth, never tempted. She wouldn't have dreamed of eating chocolate. But she knew somebody who would.

She pursued the other part of her plan by night. She often went out at night, through the cat flap. And yes, a cat can see in the dark. Crossing the side yard, she began her plan by walking beside the fence, back and forth, speaking quietly, seemingly to herself.

A dog lived on the other side. That's what the board fence was for. The Cleveland family raised it to keep their dog, Grover, penned up when they saw he'd be no good at guarding the house. Fluffy had long watched Grover from the sill of an upstairs window. She'd wondered many times if she'd ever have a use for him.

He was a young dog—about eighth grade in human terms—with big stumbling paws and a big sloppy mouth with tall teeth inside. He looked fierce, and Fluffy wondered if he might have some pit bull in him. But she'd noticed how completely he'd flunked out as a guard dog. The Clevelands had put up the fence to protect *him*. He was exactly the kind of dog who'll get out in the traffic. And of course Grover was always hungry. Dogs have no self-control. You could hear him day and night rattling his dog dish on the porch with his great wet tongue.

When it penetrated Grover's brain that a cat was stalking the far side of his fence, he began to throw himself against his side.

"That's right, that's right," Fluffy hissed softly. "I'm scared. See me tremble. What a big mean dog. I'm puss shaking in my boots."

Thus she taunted him. Cats have their own language, spoken everywhere. It comes from an ancient Egyptian tongue, and it's called *cat patois*. Dogs have their own language too. Yes, all that barking has a grammatical construction. And they have come to know enough cat patois to get by. Dogs have developed a respect for cats because brains beat brawn every time.

It took several nights to settle Grover down. Finally he was just patrolling his side of the fence as Fluffy patrolled hers. They fell into conversation, though she had to keep it simple.

"Hungry?" she inquired.

"Like all the time," Grover replied. Through the fence she could hear him panting and imagined him drooling down his chops.

"Well, you wouldn't want to eat me. I'm all bones that would stick in your throat. Care for chocolate?"

"Yeah, but, you know, it's not allowed."

Fluffy pretended surprise, even shock. "You mean the Clevelands won't give you any chocolate, even when you've been a good boy? But chocolate is absolutely delicious. I mean it's like good. You'd like it."

Grover whined his yearning. "I like it, but it's bad for me."

That was the difference between dogs and cats, as Fluffy knew. A cat wouldn't *want* anything bad for her. "I have some chocolate for you," she said sweetly.

Fluffy heard Grover stop dead. Was he sitting up, begging?

"If you were a cat, you could climb the fence and leap over. Then you could have some chocolate. But you're only a dog."

Grover whined. He'd be barking in a minute.

"But you can start digging under the fence. I can dig on this side. Then I can give you some chocolate."

At once she heard the big thorny nails on Grover's paws begin scraping away at the dirt.

"Are you in a flower bed?" she asked.

"Yard," he said.

You brainless mutt, she thought. "Well, walk along to a flower bed and dig there. The Clevelands will notice if you're tearing up their lawn."

She listened to him lope farther along the fence and start digging again. She began digging on her side too, her hindquarters high, her exquisite bottle-brush tail tall in the darkness.

A night or two later, after much work, their paws and then their noses met, under the fence. Fluffy was ready. She'd carried out four chocolate candies in her mouth. Three houses and a hotel, not that it matters. She dropped a candy just under Grover's jaw. His tongue plastered her whiskers against her snout as he lapped it up. His breath was unspeakably foul.

"Good?" she murmured.

"Real good," Grover panted.

"Melts in your mouth, not in your paw, right?" Fluffy said. "And there's more where that came from. Keep digging."

Every night she brought him more, though never more than four. Her nose nudged them under the fence onto his tongue. It wasn't pleasant for her, but it was part of the plan. Soon Grover had dug a hole big enough for his entire head. "Keep digging," Fluffy said.

Presently he was head and shoulders onto Aunt Agnes's side of the fence. A little more digging on both sides, and Grover would be at large. "Now here's the deal," Fluffy told him. "Listen up and try to remember. There's a candy mountain waiting for you if you can just get this right."

It was an ordinary afternoon with Guthrie, Blair, Wyatt, and Roxie around the Monopoly board and Fluffy at her post on the windowsill, screened by the snagged curtain. As it was late in the school year, Trumble's Troublemakers had been especially busy, conducting extra shakedowns before school closed for summer vacation.

One of Fluffy's amber eyes was on the Monopoly players, the other noticed when Trumble's Troublemakers began to infiltrate the yard outside. They flickered like shadows along the fence. The spirea bushes quivered above Troublemakers hugging the house. Taylor Trumble, beeper on belt, was moving the troops to cover front door, back door, drainpipe. After many rehearsals, this looked like the real thing to Fluffy, a mass mugging in the making.

Unnoticed, she dropped from the windowsill and darted upstairs. Nosing open the bathroom door, she made for the bathtub. She did a little balancing act on the edge of the tub and jumped from there to the high windowsill to peer out. The side yard seethed with Troublemakers. She looked for Grover on the Clevelands' side of the fence.

There he was, standing around in his own yard, not looking alert. Fluffy meowed out in a register high enough for only a dog to hear. It seemed to reach him. Grover's ears rose, and he looked around to find the hole under the fence. He appeared to be drooling.

Soon, Guthrie, Blair, and Roxie would be slipping out of front door and back, straight into the hands of the enemy. A classic ambush. Now it must be five-thirty on the nose because Fluffy heard Wyatt mounting the stairs, heading for his windowsill to shinny down that drainpipe.

Fluffy went first. She teetered a moment on the sill's very edge. Then her claws scrabbled cold metal as she shinnied down the drainpipe like a small, furry fireman down a firehouse pole. Gravity did most of it. She got herself stopped just above the nodding spirea bushes. Looking up, she saw Wyatt's small leg emerging from the bathroom window.

Then, claws out, paws wide, she dropped through the spirea bush onto the head of a Troublemaker beneath it. It was like having a twelve-pound coonskin cap dropped on your head from a great height. Fluffy's claws fastened onto surprised flesh, and dug in.

The Troublemaker (a boy) screamed like a banshee and erupted out of the spirea bush, kicking the heads of two other Troublemakers who were planning to be Wyatt's reception committee.

When Wyatt heard all this from below, he was already out the bathroom window. But he hung there from the sill, motionless, high in the air but safe from a shakedown.

The terrified Troublemaker danced screaming out into the

yard. Attached to his head with claws like staples, Fluffy hissed and spat to complete the effect.

The sudden sound came just too late to warn the other Troublemakers. Taylor Trumble was coming out of a crouch by the back steps to mug Guthrie when somebody with a cat for a head came screeching around the corner of the house.

But the boxcutter was already in Taylor's hand. Thinking fast, Taylor decided to slice Guthrie's wallet out of his jeans pocket and then take off between the two garages, leaving the rest of the gang to their fate. Sunlight glinted off the raised boxcutter when out of nowhere a huge dog came bounding across the yard, between the feet of the cat-headed screamer. The dog moved like a blur and could have been a pit bull. It made an almighty leap and its vast paws brought Taylor Trumble down. Taylor's face was jammed into a marigold border, and Grover's paws pinned Taylor in place.

It all happened too quick for Guthrie. He stood there with his green visor still on, at the foot of the back porch steps. Behind him emerged Aunt Agnes with a broom. At the sight of it, Fluffy leaped lightly down off the Troublemaker's head. She made her modest way across the grass, where she could see Grover panting hot breath on the back of terrorized Taylor's neck. Fluffy observed from a distance, one paw drawn up, like any innocent bystander.

"And what have we here?" Aunt Agnes said, stomping down the back steps. She swept Grover off Taylor's back, and Grover shied away, tail between his legs.

Cautiously, Taylor (a girl) turned over. Guthrie tried not to cower behind Aunt Agnes, who glared down at Taylor.

"Are you or are you not Taylor Trumble, daughter of Mary Louise Trumble of my church circle meeting?"

"Actually—yes," Taylor said in a small, ladylike voice.

"And what is that open blade of surgical steel doing in your hand?"

"Actually," Taylor squeaked, "I was just out to cut some wildflowers for a . . . summer bouquet."

"She lies," Guthrie said from around Aunt Agnes. "She runs the meanest gang in school. Shakedowns, muggings, you name it. We spend half our lives dodging her."

A snarl further disfigured Taylor's face. "You'll pay for that, you—"

"And what is that ridiculous ring in your nose?" Aunt Agnes said. "Your mother will chain you to the house from it after I've had a word with her."

Taylor whimpered.

Her Troublemakers had already melted away, like dew in the dawn. Taylor was a leader without followers. Her whimper dampened to a sob.

Blair and Roxie strolled arm in arm from the front of the house, not a scratch on either one of them. "There were only three of them waiting for us under the front porch," they said. "And they were boys, so we could handle them."

Then Wyatt turned up from the drainpipe.

Aunt Agnes told Guthrie to go in the house and call Mrs. Trumble. Pretty soon she arrived and led Taylor away, practically by the nose. Guthrie, Blair, Wyatt, and Roxie went on home then, freely on sidewalks.

That left Grover and Fluffy. He edged toward her, hunkering down as dogs do. "I was a good boy," he whined hopefully. "Chocolate?"

"Yes, yes," Fluffy hissed on her way to the cat flap. "I'll get back to you on that."

I Go Along

Anyway, Mrs. Tibbetts comes into the room for second period, so we all see she's still in school. She's pregnant, and the smart money says she'll make it to Easter. After that we'll have a sub teaching us. Not that we're too particular about who's up there at the front of the room, not in this class.

Being juniors, we also figure we know all there is to know about sex. We know things no adult ever heard of. Still, the sight of a pregnant English teacher slows us down some. But she's married to Roy Tibbetts, a plumber who was in the service and went to jump school, so that's okay. We see him around town in his truck.

And right away Darla Craig's hand is up. It's up a lot. She doesn't know any more English than the rest of us, but she likes to talk. "Hey, Mrs. Tibbetts, how come they get to go and we don't?"

She means the first-period people, the Advanced English class. Mrs. Tibbetts looks like Darla's caught her off base. We never hear what a teacher tells us, but we know this. At least Darla does.

"I hadn't thought." Mrs. Tibbetts rubs her hand down the small of her back, which may have something to do with being pregnant. So now we're listening, even here in the back row. "For those of you who haven't heard," she says, "I'm taking some members of the—other English class over to the college tonight, for a program."

The college is Bascomb College, a thirty-mile trip over an undivided highway.

"We're going to hear a poet read from his works."

Somebody says, "Is he living?" And we all get a big bang out of this.

But Mrs. Tibbetts just smiles. "Oh yes, he's very much alive." She reaches for her attendance book, but this sudden thought strikes her. "Would anyone in this class like to go too?" She looks up at us, and you see she's being fair, and nice.

It's only the second period of the day, so we're all feeling pretty good. Also it's a Tuesday, a terrible TV night. Everybody in class puts up their hands. Everybody. Even Marty Crawshaw, who's already married. And Pink Hohenfield, who's in class today for the first time this month. I put up mine. I go along.

Mrs. Tibbetts has never seen this many hands up in our class. She's never seen anybody's hand except Darla's. Her eyes get wide. Mrs. Tibbetts has great eyes, and she doesn't put anything on them. Which is something Darla could learn from.

But then she sees we have to be putting her on. So she just says, "Anyone who would like to go, be in the parking lot at five-thirty. And eat first. No eating on the bus."

Mrs. Tibbetts can drive the school bus. Whenever she's taking the advanced class anywhere, she can use the bus anytime she wants to, unless the coach needs it.

Then she opens her attendance book, and we tune out. And at five-thirty that night I'm in the parking lot. I have no idea why. Needless to say, I'm the only one here from second period. Marty Crawshaw and Pink Hohenfield will be out in the parking lot of Taco Bell about now, sitting on their hoods. Darla couldn't make it either. Right offhand I can't think of anybody who wants to ride a school bus thirty miles to see a poet. Including me.

The Advanced-English juniors mill around behind school. I'm still in my car, and it's almost dark, so no one sees me.

Then Mrs. Tibbetts wheels the school bus in, amber fogs flashing. She hits the brakes, and the doors fly open. The advanced class starts to climb aboard. They're more orderly than us, but they've got their groups too. And a couple of smokers.

I'm settling behind my dashboard. The last kid climbs on the bus.

And I seem to be sprinting across the asphalt. I'm on the bus, and the door's hissing shut behind me. I don't look at Mrs. Tibbetts, and she doesn't say anything. I wonder where I'm supposed to sit.

There are plenty of seats. I find an empty double and settle by the window, pulling my ball cap down in front. When we go past Taco Bell, I'm way down in the seat with my hand shielding my face on the window side. Right about then somebody sits down next to me. I flinch.

"Okay?" she says, and I look up, and it's Sharon Willis.

I've got my knees jammed up on the back of the seat ahead of me. I'm bent double, and my hand's over half my face. I'm cool, and it's Sharon Willis. "Whatever," I say.

"How are you doing, Gene?"

I'm trying to be invisible, and she's calling me by name.

"How do you know me?" I ask her.

She shifts around. "I'm a junior, you're a junior. There are about fifty-three people in our whole year. How could I not?"

Easy, I think, but don't say it. She's got a notebook on her lap. Everybody seems to, except me.

"Do you have to take notes?" I say, because I feel like I'm getting into something here.

"Not really," Sharon says, "but we have to write about it in class tomorrow. Our impressions."

I'm glad I'm not in her class, because I'm not going to have any impressions. Here I am on the school bus for the Gifted with the major goddess girl in school, who knows my name. I'm going to be clean out of impressions because my circuits are already starting to fail.

Sharon and I don't turn this into anything. When the bus gets out on the route and Mrs. Tibbetts puts the pedal to the metal, we settle back. Sharon's more or less in with the top group of girls around school. They're not even cheerleaders. They're a notch above that. The rest of them are up and down the aisle, but she stays put. Michelle Burkholder sticks her face down by Sharon's ear and says, "We've got a seat for you back here."

But Sharon just says, "I'll stay here with Gene." Like it happens every day.

I look out the window a lot. When we get close to the campus of Bascomb College, I think about staying on the bus. "Do you want to sit together," Sharon says, "at the program?"

I clear my throat. "You go ahead and sit with your people."

"I sit with them all day long," she says.

At Bascomb College we're up on bleachers in a curtained-off part of the gym. Mrs. Tibbetts says we can sit anywhere, so we get very groupy. I look around, and here I am in these bleachers, like we've gone to State in the play-offs. And I'm just naturally here with Sharon Willis.

We're surrounded mainly by college students. Sharon has her notebook open. I figure it's going to be like a class, so I'm tuning out when the poet comes on.

First of all, he's probably only in his twenties. Not even a beard, and he's not dressed like a poet. In fact, he's dressed like me: Levi's and Levi's jacket. Big heavy-duty belt buckle. Boots, even. A tall guy, about a hundred and eighty pounds. It's weird, like there could be poets around and you wouldn't realize they were there.

But he's got something. Every girl leans forward. College girls, even. Michelle Burkholder bobs up to zap him with her digital camera. He's got a few loose-leaf pages in front of him. But he just begins.

"I've written a poem for my wife," he says, "about her."

Then he tells us this poem. I'm waiting for the rhyme, but it's more like talking, about how he wakes up and the sun's bright on the bed and his wife's still asleep. He watches her.

"Alone," he says, "I watch you sleep
Before the morning steals you from me.
Before you stir and disappear
Into the day and leave me here
to turn and kiss the warm space
You leave beside me."

He looks up and people clap. I thought what he said was a little too personal, but I could follow it. Next to me Sharon's made a note. I look down at her page and see it's just an exclamation point.

He tells us a lot of poems, one after another. I mean, he's got poems on everything. He even has one about his truck:

"Old Buck-toothed, slow-to-start mama,"

something like that. People laugh, which I guess is okay. He just keeps at it, and he really jerks us around with his poems. I mean, you don't know what the next one's going to be about. They bring him a glass of water, and he takes a break, but mainly he keeps going.

He ends up with one called "High School."

> *"On my worst nights," he says, "I dream myself back.*
> *I'm the hostage in the row by the radiator, boxed in,*
> *Zit-blasted, and they're popping quizzes at me.*
> *I'm locked in there, looking for words*
> *To talk myself out of being this young*
> *While every girl in the galaxy*
> *Is looking over my head, spotting for a senior.*
> *On my really worst nights it's last period*
> *On a Friday and somebody's fixed the bell*
> *So it won't ring:*
> > *And I've been cut from the team,*
> > *And I've forgotten my locker combination,*
> > *And I'm waiting for something damn it to hell*
> > *To happen."*

And the crowd goes wild, especially the college people. The poet just gives us a wave and walks over to sit down on the bottom bleacher. People swarm him to sign their programs. Except Sharon and I stay where we are.

"That last one wasn't a poem," I tell her. "The others were, but not that one."

She turns to me and smiles. I've never been close enough to see the color of her eyes before. "Then write a better one," she says.

We're still sitting together on the ride home.

"No, I'm serious," I say. "You can't write poems about zits and your locker combinations."

"Maybe nobody told the poet that," Sharon says.

"So what are you going to write about him tomorrow?" I'm really curious about this.

"I don't know," she says. "I've never heard a poet in person. Mrs. Tibbetts shows us tapes of poets reading."

"She doesn't show them to our class."

"What would you do if she did?" Sharon asks.

"Laugh a lot."

The bus settles down on the return trip. I picture these people going home to do algebra homework, or whatever. When Sharon speaks again, I almost don't hear her.

"You ought to be in this class," she says.

I jerk my cap down to my nose and lace my fingers behind my head and kick back in the seat. Which should be answer enough.

"You're as bright as anybody on this bus. Brighter than some."

We're rolling through the night, and I can't believe I'm

hearing this. It's dark, so I chance a glance at her. Just the out-line of her nose and her chin, maybe a little stubborn.

"How do you know I am?"

"How do you know you're not?" she says. "How will you ever know?"

But then we're quiet because what else is there to say? And anyway, the evening's over. Mrs. Tibbetts is braking for the turnoff, and we're about to get back to normal. And I get this quick flash of tomorrow, in second period with Marty and Pink and Darla, and frankly it doesn't look that good.

The Kiss in the
Carry-on Bag

I

Seb woke to find his feet were out of the covers, cooling. At the
window, birds bickered. But the rest of the world seemed to be
waiting.

He wasn't a morning kind of guy, even with a full night's
sleep. He had a problem with that quick shift from dreams to
the truth. Moments ago he'd been having his dream about the
customized, stretched Range Rover. And where the backseat

had been was a hot tub. And Seb himself is in the hot tub with a couple of—

Then gray morning.

He'd gone out last night. It was meant to feel spur-of-the-moment, but they'd planned. Things always had to be planned. Seb and Pauli and Rudy went out. Nothing special. Just out.

Pauli and Rudy came over and dressed at Seb's place, of course. Not Levi's and muscle shirts—a step up from that, cool but low-key. Rudy used to have a stud in his tongue. But it worked loose, and he'd swallowed it. Though he'd looked for it, he never found it.

So no metal, on any of them. Pauli had brought Seb a pair of dark, wraparound glasses. They all worked a little bit on their hair, then they went out. You could walk anywhere from Seb's place.

So then what? They thought about a movie, but they'd have to buck the line. They decided not to, not for Bruce Willis. Though it was early for a club, they swung past Airheads. The doorman, Paco, knew Pauli and never asked questions. They were in there if they wanted to be. But it meant bucking another line. They moved on.

They went here. They went there. Seb didn't even remember. He wasn't exactly cursed with total recall, as his old teachers used to say. And French grammar? Forget about it. Geography? Seb could barely find his way home.

They ended up at a new Internet cafe, just for a latte. You

could see the whole place from the street—mostly glowing
screens and a coffee bar where you picked up your own order.
While Pauli and Rudy went to the counter, Seb sank into a
deep armchair and scanned the room. A few people on line,
a few more clustered around little tables. No familiar faces—
not that kind of place.

One minute he's gazing mindless around the room. The
next minute this girl is there, right by his shoulder, looking
down. Seb looked up. Everything began to look up. She was on
the border of beautiful. And very, very close. Closer than
any—

"I've just e-mailed everybody I ever knew," she said. "Why
send postcards, right? You get home before they do. I don't
even know where you buy stamps in this country."

". . . Ah," Seb said.

"You on-line a lot?" the girl asked.

". . . Not a lot," Seb said.

She had a fall of burnished red-brown hair. Like chestnuts
by firelight, thought Seb, who had become this sudden poet.

"Oh. You're foreign," she said. "I mean, no, you're not. I'm
foreign, right? You live here."

"All my life," Seb said.

"I could tell," she said, "because of your accent."

"But you're the one with the accent," Seb said.

"No, I'm not," the girl said. "I'm from Indiana. We don't
have an accent. We just have a little bit of a twang. *You've* got
an accent."

He had to keep her talking. For one thing, she had a wonderful accent. She had wonderful—

She glanced at the other two chairs. The one for Pauli, the
one for Rudy.

"I'm alone," Seb said. "Would you like to sit down?"

He started up out of the chair, but she put a hand on his
shoulder. Then when she'd sat down across from him, he
could still feel where her hand had been.

"Before I realized you were foreign—from here, I thought
you might go to Park-Tudor," she said. "I figured you for private school. You know. Very blond. Probably tall. And you
paid too much for the jacket."

Seb looked down himself. When he looked up again, the
girl had leaned nearer. In a lower voice she said, "Personally,
I'd ditch the shades. Wraparounds are so out. Especially after
dark. Especially indoors."

She spoke like a spy. A lovely, lovely spy.

"Ah," Seb said. "I think I'll keep the glasses on."

"You're like the guys at my school," she said. "They probably wear their ball caps to bed. It's a security issue, right?"

". . . Right," Seb said. But now here came Pauli and Rudy,
with the lattes. They saw her. Seb shook his head. They
swerved to another table.

"I'm Ally, by the way," she said.

"I'm Seb."

"You're kidding."

"Sebastian, actually."

"Oh, that's too bad." For one perfect moment Seb thought she might reach out and touch his knee. "But then my real name is Alicia Mae. I was named for my grandmother."

"So was I," Seb breathed.

"You had a grandmother named Sebastian?" Ally's eyes were huge.

"No. I mean. It was my grandfather's . . ."

But now she was smiling, grinning really. "You blush," she said. "It's like a sunset."

His face was hot. Strobing. From the other table, Pauli and Rudy watched like hawks.

Seb stirred, cracking a knee on the low table. "Would you like something?" he said. "A latte?"

He'd made it to his feet. He actually was tall, to his great relief.

"Whatever," she said, looking up at him.

"How do you like it? Your latte?" Was that what you asked? His head pounded.

"You decide," she said.

But Seb never decided things. He turned blindly in the room. Pauli and Rudy sat hunched at a table between him and the counter.

"She wants a latte," he whispered, dipping down to them, desperate.

"Is she an American girl?" Pauli muttered, watching her back.

"Yes."

"Better do as she says," Rudy said. "They expect that. Just go up to the counter and—"

"But I don't have any money," Seb said, low and hopeless. "You know that."

Pauli and Rudy had hardly touched their lattes. "Here, give me those." Seb swept them up. Careful not to spill a drop, he bore them away.

"That was quick." Ally looked up. She was all in black. Who wasn't? But on her it worked. "You ought to be a waiter. But that's the only tip you get."

Seb stared down, openmouthed at everything about her.

"That was like a joke," she said. "Just sit down." After the first sip, she said, "I think I've got you totally figured."

Doomed, Seb supposed.

"Correct me if I'm wrong," Ally said. "You're—what, seventeen, sort of?"

Seb nodded.

"Me too, practically," she said. "I'll be a senior. And all the guys at school are really, really immature, you know? But you—you're like younger than they are."

Seb sank back, relieved. Shattered.

"And I bet I know why." Ally lasered him with a look. "You go to an all-boys school, am I right?"

Seb nodded. "I did. You saw right through me."

"Did? You've finished school?"

"School is finished with me." He didn't explain. He had his pride. "This place where you live, this Indiana," he said to change the subject. "How big a city is it?"

Now her eyes were enormous. "City? It's a whole state.

Like—the United *States,* okay? It's only about four times the size of this whole country of yours."

". . . Ah," Seb said. Ally had a white mustache now, from latte foam and double whipped cream, the way Rudy liked it. Chestnut hair, enormous eyes, white mustache. Seb felt faint.

She was telling him about this school "study tour" of Europe her class was on. They allowed three days for each country. The next stop was Norway, or Luxembourg, one of those.

"And you've enjoyed my country?" Seb strained to hit his stride.

"It's really small," Ally said. "Everybody in our group keeps bumping their heads. But it's nice." She dropped her voice and leaned nearer. "Though just between you and me, I'll never need to see another moat."

". . . Moat?" Seb began to drown in her eyes.

"Moat," Ally said. "You know. That wet area around castles."

Does she like me a little? he wondered.

"Are you seeing anybody?" she asked.

Through these glasses he was straining to see *her.*

"Like are you going out with anybody? A girl?"

Seb couldn't get it together. Ally was wearing some kind of perfume or something.

"Do you *know* any girls?"

". . . Not really," Seb said. "But there's this one girl. Her family . . . my family . . . we've always known each other."

"Oh, right," Ally said. "One of those deals. What's her name?"

"Irmgard."

"Oh, that's too bad." Now she did reach out and touch his knee. But then she checked her watch. "Listen, I've got to get back to the dorm. Your buses stop running at midnight."

"They do?"

Her eyes were huge again. "Hello. You don't get out much, do you? You must have been in a boarding school. This is the capital of the country, and it shuts down at night like Kokomo."

"Oh," Seb said. She was on her feet now, dabbing off her mustache. At their table Pauli and Rudy stirred.

Seb remembered to hold the door for her. After a light rain, the cobblestones gleamed like little moons. A historic building across the street leaned quaintly over the pavement. "Shall I walk you to where the bus stops?" Seb's hand and hers brushed.

"Do you *know* where the bus stops?"

". . . No."

Ally pointed the way. A few people were up on ladders, draping streetlamps with flags in the national colors.

"Tomorrow's a holiday, right?" Ally said.

"Right," Seb said.

"There'll be a parade?" Her hand brushed his again.

Lightning struck in Seb's brain. Was she hinting that maybe they could watch the parade together? He panicked. "I can't," he blurted. "I'm . . . all tied up."

"Whatever," Ally said, and the bus loomed. Too soon, too soon. "And the next day we leave."

"For Norway," Seb said bleakly.

"Probably."

The bus doors wheezed open. She had one foot on the step when she looked back. "Tell me one last thing."

He'd tell her anything now.

"Do those other two guys follow you everywhere?"

The doors closed, and the bus lumbered away. Seb turned back to a large stone pillar. Behind it would be Pauli and Rudy.

But all that was last night. Ally had since morphed into being both girls in Seb's hot tub dream. Now it was gray dawn. The birds were gone, but something stirred. A shuffling noise came from below the window, the sound of a lot of feet. Seb braced himself in bed.

Then in an ear-splitting explosion, a full brass band struck up. The courtyard echoed and bellowed. The brass drum throbbed. Bagpipes whined. Cymbals crashed. It was deafening. The band had burst into HAPPY BIRTHDAY TO YOU.

The full choir of the National Cathedral erupted into song: HAPPY BIRTHDAY, QUEEN MOTHER, HAPPY BIRTHDAY TO YOU!

Seb grabbed his head.

It was a national holiday because this was the Queen Mother's big birthday. She was a hundred years old today. So of course it was a national holiday, but it wasn't a day off for Seb. Because Seb was the Queen Mother's great-grandson.

And heir to the throne.

II

Three rousing cheers rose from the courtyard, to wish the Queen Mother, rather unnecessarily, long life. As the last cheer died away, Seb's bedroom door flung open.

They never knock, he thought. They barge in like this is public property. Though being a palace, it probably was.

They were here in force this morning. In came the aged Head Deputy Master of the Royal Household. "Your Royal Highness," he said, giving Seb his first bow of the day.

Behind him came Seb's valet. After a quick bow, he backed into the bathroom to draw Seb's bath. The barber bowed in and backed to the bathroom after him. You couldn't turn your back on royalty, so there were a lot of people Seb had only seen from the front. Two footmen brought in his breakfast, under silver covers.

Then a beat behind, Seb's lords-in-waiting—his equerries—jostled each other through the door. They were in double-breasted suits, and their shoes were polished to mirrors. But one equerry's necktie was practically around his ear. And the other one in his haste had buttoned up his suit jacket wrong. He seemed to list to starboard. They were Viscount Crickle-mere and the Baron of Budleigh.

Pauli and Rudy.

His Royal Highness, the Prince Sebastian, sat in the carriage beside His Royal Highness, the Prince Reginald—Seb's little brother, Reggie. Seb and Reggie sat backward, across from the Queen Mother, who took up much of her seat. It was her personal state carriage, gold with cupids.

The parade got a late start. Seb and Reggie had been dressed, brushed down, and delivered on time. The King and Queen, their parents, already sat in the carriage with roll-up windows so if they started in on each other, the public couldn't hear it. The King and Queen appeared together only on national holidays and postage stamps.

The Queen Mother herself had held up the show. She was just being hoisted up into the Cupid Carriage when the old dear remembered she'd forgotten her cough medicine. So stop the world. She went nowhere without it, carried in a silver flask inside her giant handbag. She was deaf as a post, but had a tongue in her head, and she wasn't going anywhere without her cough medicine. Footmen were sent.

Seb and Reggie could only sit there, smelling the horses. The Queen Mother looked suspiciously around under a hat the size of a satellite dish. Her mammoth handbag slid off her knees. Reggie reached down to get it for her, but Great-granny was quicker. She snatched up the handbag and gave him a sharp clout across the ear with it.

"Yeow!" Reggie exclaimed.

"And you're supposed to be the smart one?" Seb remarked. "Even I know not to mess with her when her flask's missing."

It was said that while Seb would inherit the throne, Reggie had inherited the brains. Who from, Seb couldn't imagine. At ten, Reggie seemed nowhere near puberty, but he talked like a dictionary. He went to a special Swiss school for Gifted Royalty who were reading on grade level.

The day was warming up, and the horse smells were getting to be unbearable. "Why do we have to go through this?" Seb sulked. "I could be—"

"Because you are the Heir Apparent, Seb," Reggie explained in his high, annoying voice. "And I am the Heir Presumptive. We're the Heir and the Spare. When Daddy pops off, you'll be King, and I'll be—"

"Beheaded," Seb muttered.

The flask was handed up, and Great-granny's gloved claw grabbed it out of the air. Unscrewing the lid, she knocked back a shot, and the Cupid Carriage began to roll.

The parade ahead of them had been going on for some time. Every marching band in the kingdom marched. Then came the Royal Navy, with oars, and most of the army, on foot, displaying their only Hummer. Footballers marched in their shorts. The Royal Girl Guides pulled a float like a giant birthday cake with a hundred candles, unlit to prevent a firestorm.

After a drum and bugle corps passed by, the Cupid Carriage clattered out of the palace yard, behind plumed horses, toward the roaring crowds. Cameras flashed, and Great-granny snapped to, becoming the Queen Mother. Her gloved hand, rattling diamonds, came up, and she gave her roaring subjects her sweetest smile.

The breeze stirred the plumes on her stupendous hat. "Like a grenade going off in an ostrich farm," Seb muttered. Reggie was practicing his nod and his wave, like a little wind-up prince-doll. Seb slumped.

A heavy foot in a large high-heeled shoe shot out from under Great-granny's skirts and connected with Seb's ankle. "Give them a grin, you little git," she snapped, smiling in her modest way at the crowds.

So Seb had to pull himself together and play Prince.

He gave the crowds a small smile and shoulder-level wave. When he ran a hand through his hair, several girls in school uniforms, perched on a wall, shrieked.

"Who *are* those silly girls?" Reggie looked around at him. "Could they have been cheering for you, Seb?"

"I wondered about that," Seb admitted modestly.

"They must be brain-dead," Reggie said.

With the hand that wasn't waving, Great-granny unscrewed the cap on her flask.

III

Cassandra Conway clung to the top of an ornamental fountain. Surrounded by spouting dolphins, the fountain stood in the capital's central square, the best place in town for watching the parade. Cassandra usually managed the best place for herself.

Clinging just below her was her more-or-less best friend,

Ally Bidwell. The footballers of the Royal Playing Fields Alliance marching in their shorts had brightened Cassandra's day. But the parade was in a lull after them—large girls dragging a plastic birthday cake. Cassandra and Ally clung to the top of the fountain above a sea of fluttering handheld flags.

"Could you kill for a Big Mac?" Cassandra said down to Ally. The capitals of Europe blazed with Golden Arches. But the American embassy had warned them against ground beef.

"Cass, get your boot off my shoulder," Ally said. They'd been dorm-mates on this trip through seven countries. Things were growing thin between them. At home, Cass had her own bathroom.

"Honestly, look at those dorky girls pulling that bogus birthday cake."

"Cass, shut up," Ally said. "We're not supposed to act like ugly Americans until we get home."

A drum and bugle corps passed endlessly by. Then behind feathery horses came a knockout of a solid-gold carriage, with cupids. Spoke wheels. Footmen with powdered wigs. The works.

"Here she comes," Cass cried, "the old woman!"

"I believe she's called the Queen Mother," Ally said.

"Whatever. Yikes, can you see her hat? It's like a giant auk. And who are those two with her. Are they like the princes?" Cass hung far out from the fountain. "Oh, wow," she said. "Look at the big one!"

A well-timed sunbeam struck Seb's blond hair. He'd picked up the shy smile from Great-granny. He was perfecting her backhand wave. Cass nearly pitched off her pinnacle. "What are their names?" she yelled down to Ally.

"I don't know about the little one," Ally said. "But the big one's Seb."

"Seb?"

"I think I had a latte with him last night."

"In your dreams," Cass called down.

"No. For sure. He looks just like the guy I—"

"You wish, Jack," Cass replied.

By chance, Seb's gaze swept the top of the fountain where two foreign girls clung, one on top of the other. The top one hung far out into space. It was the one she was standing on who caught Seb's attention.

He lurched, and Reggie thought he might leap to his feet. "Don't upstage Great-granny unless you want a thick ear," Reggie advised. Seb subsided.

But his eyes met hers. It was—

"Ally!" Seb called, loud over the crowd, though Great-granny wouldn't hear.

"Hey, Seb!" Ally yelled back. "How about a latte?"

Cass swayed. Her parents had laid out three grand for this trip, and it was *Ally* who got to meet a prince? Cass felt like both of the ugly stepsisters in *Cinderella*. She ground a boot heel into Ally's shoulder.

But Ally didn't feel a thing because as the gold carriage passed below, Seb blew her a kiss.

Seventy girls in the central square vicinity blew kisses back.

But it was a kiss for Ally, and she knew it. She only nodded down to Seb, a little mock bow for His Royal Highness or whatever, and sent him a smile she hoped he'd keep in mind.

He was still looking back as the carriage went by.

And in her carry-on bag of souvenirs, Ally tucked away a first kiss from a prince. True, he'd had to hurl it fifty feet. Cass said it didn't count.

Ally said, excuse me, but it did.

The Three-Century Woman

"I guess if you live long enough," my mom said to Aunt Gloria, "you get your fifteen minutes of fame."

Mom was on the car phone to Aunt Gloria. The minute
Mom rolls out of the garage, she's on her car phone. It's state-
of-the-art and better than her car.

We were heading for Whispering Oaks to see my great-
grandmother Breckenridge, who's lived there since I was a little girl. They call it an Elder Care Facility. Needless to say, I
hated going.

The reason for Great-grandma's fame is that she was born in 1899. Now it's January 2001. If you're one of those people who claim the new century begins in 2001, not 2000, even you have to agree that Great-grandma Breckenridge has lived in three centuries. This is her claim to fame.

We waited for a light to change along by Northbrook Mall, and I gazed fondly over at it. Except for the Multiplex, it was closed because of New Year's Day. I have a severe mall habit. But I'm fourteen, and the mall is the place without homework. Aunt Gloria's voice filled the car.

"If you take my advice," she told Mom, "you'll keep those Whispering Oaks people from letting the media in to interview Grandma. Interview her my foot! Honestly. She doesn't know where she is, let alone how many centuries she's lived in. The poor old soul. Leave her in peace. She's already got one foot in the—"

"Gloria, your trouble is you have no sense of history." Mom gunned across the intersection. "You got a C in history."

"I was sick a lot of that year," Aunt Gloria said.

"Sick of history," Mom mumbled.

"I heard that," Aunt Gloria said.

They bickered on, but I tuned them out. Then when we turned in at Whispering Pines, a sound truck from IBC-TV was blocking the drive.

"Good grief," Mom murmured. "TV."

"I told you," Aunt Gloria said, but Mom switched her off. She parked in a frozen rut.

"I'll wait in the car," I said. "I have homework."

"Get out of the car," Mom said.

If you get so old you have to be put away, Whispering Oaks isn't that bad. It smells all right, and a Christmas tree glittered in the lobby. A real tree. On the other hand, you have to push a red button to unlock the front door. I guess it's to keep the inmates from escaping, though Great-grandma Breckenridge wasn't going anywhere and hadn't for twenty years.

When we got to her wing, the hall was full of camera crews and a woman from the suburban newspaper with a notepad.

Mom sighed. It was like that first day of school when you think you'll be okay until the teachers learn your name. Stepping over a cable, we stopped at Great-grandma's door, and they were on to us.

"Who are you people to Mrs. Breckenridge?" the newspaper-woman said. "I want names."

These people were seriously pushy. And the TV guy was wearing more makeup than Mom. It dawned on me that they couldn't get into Great-grandma's room without her permission. Mom turned on them.

"Listen, you're not going to be interviewing my grandmother," she said in a quiet bark. "I'll be glad to tell you anything you want to know about her, but you're not going in there. She's got nothing to say, and . . . she needs a lot of rest."

"Is it Alzheimer's?" the newswoman asked. "Because we're thinking Alzheimer's."

"Think what you want," Mom said. "But this is as far as you get. And you people with the camera and the light, you're not going in there either. You'd scare her to death, and then I'd sue the pants off you."

They pulled back.

But a voice came wavering out of Great-grandma's room. Quite an eerie, echoing voice.

"Let them in!" the voice said.

It had to be Great-grandma Breckenridge. Her roommate had died. "Good grief," Mom muttered, and the press surged forward.

Mom and I went in first, and our eyes popped. Great-grandma was usually flat out in the bed, dozing, with her teeth in a glass and a book in her hand. Today she was bright-eyed and propped up. She wore a fuzzy pink bed jacket. A matching bow was stuck in what remained of her hair.

"Oh, for pity's sake," Mom said. "They've got her done up like a Barbie doll."

Great-grandma peered from the bed at Mom. "And who are you?" she asked.

"I'm Ann," Mom said carefully. "This is Megan," she said, meaning me.

"That's right," Great-grandma said. "At least you know who you are. Plenty around this place don't."

The guy with the camera on his shoulder barged in. The other guy turned on a blinding light.

Great-grandma blinked. In the glare we noticed she wore a trace of lipstick. The TV anchor elbowed the woman reporter aside and stuck a mike in Great-grandma's face. Her claw hand came out from under the covers and tapped it.

"It this thing on?" she inquired.

"Yes, ma'am," the TV anchor said in his broadcasting voice. "Don't you worry about all this modern technology. We don't understand half of it ourselves." He gave her his big, five-thirty news smile and settled on the edge of her bed. There was room for him. She was tiny.

"We're here to congratulate you for having lived in three centuries—for being a Three-Century Woman! A great achievement!"

Great-grandma waved a casual claw. "Nothing to it," she said. "You sure this mike's on? Let's do this in one take."

The cameraman snorted and moved in for a closer shot. Mom stood still as a statue, wondering what was going to come out of Great-grandma's mouth next.

"Mrs. Breckenridge," the anchor said, "to what do you attribute your long life?"

"I was only married once," Great-grandma said. "And he died young."

The anchor stared. "Ah. And anything else?"

"Yes. I don't look back. I live in the present."

The camera panned around the room. This was all the present she had, and it didn't look like much.

"You live for the present," the anchor said, looking for an angle, "even now?"

Great-grandma nodded. "Something's always happening. Last night I fell off the bed pan."

Mom groaned.

The cameraman pulled in for a tighter shot. The anchor seemed to search his mind. You could tell he thought he was a great interviewer, though he had no sense of humor. A tiny smile played around Great-grandma's wrinkled lips.

"But you've lived through amazing times, Mrs. Breckenridge. And you never think back about them?"

Great-grandma stroked her chin and considered. "You mean you want to hear something interesting? Like how I lived through the San Francisco earthquake—the big one of oh-six?"

Beside me, Mom stirred. We were crowded over by the dead lady's bed. "You survived the 1906 San Francisco earthquake?" the anchor said.

Great-grandma gazed at the ceiling, lost in thought.

"I'd have been about seven years old. My folks and I were staying at that big hotel. You know the one. I slept in a cot at the foot of their bed. In the middle of the night, that room gave a shake, and the chiffonier walked right across the floor. You know what a chiffonier is?"

"A chest of drawers?" the anchor said.

"Close enough," Great-grandma said. "And the pictures flapped on the walls. We had to walk down twelve flights because the elevators didn't work. When we got outside, the streets were ankle-deep in broken glass. You never saw such a mess in your life."

Mom nudged me and hissed: "She's never been to San Francisco. She's never been west of Denver. I've heard her say so."

"Incredible!" the anchor said.

"Truth's stranger than fiction," Great-grandma said, smoothing her sheet.

"And you never think back about it?"

Great-grandma shrugged her little fuzzy pink shoulders. "I've been through too much. I don't have time to remember it all. I was on the *Hindenburg* when it blew up, you know."

Mom moaned, and the cameraman was practically standing on his head for a close-up.

"The *Hindenburg*?"

"That big gas thing the Germans built to fly over the Atlantic Ocean. It was called a zeppelin. Biggest thing you ever saw—five city blocks long. It was in May of 1937, before your time. You wouldn't remember. My husband and I were coming back from Europe. No, wait a minute."

Great-grandma cocked her head and pondered for the camera.

"My husband was dead by then. It was some other man. Anyway, the two of us were coming back on the *Hindenburg*. It was smooth as silk. You didn't know you were moving. When we flew in over New York, they stopped the ball game at Yankee Stadium to see us passing overhead."

Great-grandma paused, caught up in the memories.

"And then the *Hindenburg* exploded," the anchor said, prompting her.

She nodded. "We had no complaints about the trip till then. The luggage was all stacked, and we were coming in at Lakehurst, New Jersey. I was wearing my beige coat—beige or off-white, I forget. Then whoosh! The gondola heated up like an oven, and people peeled out of the windows. We hit the ground and bounced. When we hit again, the door fell off, and I walked out and kept going. When they caught up to me in the parking lot, they wanted to put me in the hospital. I looked down and thought I was wearing a lace dress. The fire had about burned up my coat. And I lost a shoe."

"Fantastic!" the anchor breathed. "What detail!" Behind him the woman reporter was scribbling away on her pad.

"Never," Mom muttered. "Never in her life."

"Ma'am, you are living history!" the anchor said. "In your sensational span of years you've survived two great disasters!"

"Three." Great-grandma patted the bow on her head. "I told you I'd been married."

"And before we leave this venerable lady," the anchor said, flashing a smile for the camera, "we'll ask Mrs. Breckenridge if she has any predictions for this new twenty-first century ahead of us here in the Dawn of the Millennium."

"Three or four predictions," Great-grandma said, and paused again, stretching out her airtime. "Number one, taxes will be higher. Number two, it's going to be harder to find a place to park. And number three, a whole lot of people are going to live as long as I have, so get ready for us."

"And with those wise words," the anchor said, easing off the bed, "we leave Mrs. B—"

"And one more prediction," she said. "TV's on the way out. Your network ratings are already in the basement. It's all websites now. Son, I predict you'll be looking for work."

And that was it. The light went dead. The anchor, looking shaken, followed his crew out the door. When TV's done with you, they're done with you. "Is that a wrap?" Great-grandma asked.

But now the woman from the suburban paper was moving in on her. "Just a few more questions, Mrs. Breckenridge."

"Where you from?" Great-grandma blinked pink-eyed at her.

"The Glenview Weekly Shopper."

"You bring a still photographer with you?" Great-grandma asked.

"Well, no."

"And you never learned shorthand either, did you?"

"Well, no."

"Honey, I only deal with professionals. There's the door."

So then it was just Mom and Great-grandma and I in the room. Mom planted a hand on her hip. "Grandma. Number one, you've never been to San Francisco. And number two, you never *saw* one of those zeppelin things."

Great-grandma shrugged. "No, but I can read." She nodded to the pile of books on her nightstand with her spectacles folded on top. "You can pick up all that stuff in books."

"And number three," Mom said, "your husband didn't die young. I can *remember* Grandpa Breckenridge."

"It was that TV dude in the five-hundred-dollar suit who set me off," Great-grandma said. "He dyes his hair, did you notice? He made me mad, and it put my nose out of joint. He didn't notice I'm still here. He thought I was nothing but my memories. So I gave him some."

Now Mom and I stood beside her bed.

"I'll tell you something else," Great-grandma said. "And it's no lie."

We waited, holding our breath to hear. Great-grandma Breckenridge was pointing her little old bent finger right at me. "You, Megan," she said. "Once upon a time, I was your age. How scary is that?"

Then she hunched up her little pink shoulders and winked at me. She grinned and I grinned. She was just this little withered-up leaf of a lady in the bed. But I felt like giving her a kiss on her little wrinkled cheek, so I did.

"I'll come and see you more often," I told her.

"Call first," she said. "I might be busy." Then she dozed.

How to Write a Short Story

You saw something today that would make a short story. I did.

I was flying back home to New York this afternoon, in the aisle seat. We were buckled up for the approach over Manhattan island and that curve across water to LaGuardia Airport. How many times have I made that trip with nothing more in mind than wanting to get on the ground and in a cab and home? Today, I looked aside at the man in the window seat, and he was crying. His hand was over his eyes, and his face was wet with tears. I looked past him, and we were flying directly over the site of the World Trade Center. Its empty footprint.

I don't know his story, and I couldn't ask. I'm not the TV guy with the thrusting mike, trying to interview Great-grandma Breckenridge in "The Three-Century Woman."

I write fiction—novels and, as you know, short stories. I go away and think about that moment on a plane. I think about the man next to me, about his life and his laptop and what he'd lost. What we all had lost.

My mental files are full of such moments, and other people's memories. Some of them hark back to childhood, still offering up the voices and the settings of "Shotgun Cheatham's Last Night Above Ground" and "By Far the Worst Pupil at Long Point School."

Fiction isn't a press release (however inaccurate). It isn't real life with the names changed. You don't write about your grandma. You write about the grandma you wish you'd had. Fiction isn't what is; it's what if?

What if the man beside me on the plane had turned and spoken? How would I have answered?

There may be a story in that, someday when I'm not so near tears myself. If there is, I'll make it as real as I can, with special care about the voices. But it won't be anything that actually happened. It will have a different shape, a beginning, a middle, an end. At the end change will have taken place. That's all I know so far.

Something in the real world jogs or jars, and you tuck it away. We write from observation, not experience. It's easier to write about other people, maybe because you can see all the way around them, and the backs of their heads.

I was a kid once, listening to my aunt Geneva tell me about the first time she glimpsed the great world, at the world's fair of 1904. And so a half century later I could write "The Electric Summer."

I was a teacher once, and that's when I met Gene in "I Go Along," except he didn't get on the bus. From my teaching days, lockers still slam in my brain, and in "Priscilla and the Wimps."

You saw something today too. What was it?

Five Helpful Hints

There's no magic formula, no shortcut to writing the short story. Here are five hints to help you on your way, though. They help me.

HINT #1:
NOBODY BUT A READER EVER BECAME A WRITER

You have to read a thousand stories before you can write one. And of course you want to. We write by the light of every story we ever read. Reading other people's stories shows you the way to your own. You learn how a story shapes and speaks and sums up by seeing how other writers do it. Writers then. Writers now.

The short story has a long and proud tradition, without going all the way back to papyrus and Parables. It's a form that has flourished in American writing. Some say the first American short story was Washington Irving's "Rip van Winkle" in 1819. Bret Harte called the short story "the germ of American literature to come."*

To examine our roots, we read Irving and Harte, and Mark Twain's "The Celebrated Jumping Frog of Calaveras County" and William Faulkner's "A Rose for Emily" and Ring Lardner's "Haircut" and Ernest Hemingway's "Hills like White Elephants" and lots of Edgar Allan Poe and O. Henry. To see what the writers of the mid-twentieth century did to the short story form we read Eudora Welty and Flannery O'Connor and Truman Capote.

And of course we read what's being written—and published—in our own time. I'm inspired by the short stories of my friends and writing colleagues: Chris Crutcher's *Athletic Shorts* and Graham Salisbury's *Island Boyz* and from England Philippa Pearce's collection *Familiar and Haunting*.

There aren't as many magazines using short stories as there once were. But after the magazine *Cicada* reprinted my "I Go Along," I began to read every issue for its short fiction.

Cornhill Magazine, July 1899

It's too important a hint not to repeat: Nobody but a reader ever became a writer. We learn to write from the faculty of one another.

That was a long hint. Here's a shorter one. It too involves reading, research.

HINT #2:
KNOW THE MARKETS FOR SHORT STORIES

There are annual market guides to tell writers what sources publish short fiction, and what kind of stories they're looking for.

One of them is *The Market Guide for Young Writers: Where and How to Sell What You Write* by Kathy Henderson. Some guides also give information about writing contests open to young writers.

Even if you're not ready to submit your own work, these guides show the way to what is being published currently. Without knowing that, you're flying blind. Libraries keep up-to-date files of these guides.

Now a somewhat longer hint, very important:

HINT #3:
THE ONLY WRITING IS REWRITING

Everything written has to be a well-wrapped package readers can hold in their hands. Stories are shapes. For me, that means never showing anybody my first five drafts. The only writing is rewriting, and I write each of my novels, each of my stories, six times because I can't get them well wrapped in the first five tries.

I don't create a neat enough package in the early drafts. I use two words when one will do. I repeat. I don't have all the connections. I haven't tied all the threads, and I have some threads not worth tying.

The short story "By Far the Worst Pupil at Long Point School" is held together by a two-word phrase spoken three times: "I do." In the beginning, the story seems to be about Uncle Billy, who never misses a meal. Then it seems to be about Grandma, who was once the teenaged teacher of a one-room school. In fact the story is about somebody else hiding in plain sight on every line and even signaled in the title.

Before I began writing, I knew that Grandma would marry Charlie. It was only in the third draft that I discovered the repetition of "I do" that draws the story together to hand over to the reader.

Be too proud to show anybody, including a teacher, your rough drafts. Real writing isn't e-mail.

And another hint at the heart of the matter:

HINT #4:
A STORY IS ONLY AS STRONG
AS THE VOICES TELLING IT

And I'm tempted to add: The only voice a story never needs is the author's. Characters need to speak for themselves in their own distinct voices. This isn't television. Characters aren't identified by sight, but by sound. Particularly in a short story, every word they speak needs to sound like the speaker and move the story along.

Young voices and old, foreign and familiar, voices from the past and the present. Charlotte's ripe, old-fashioned British accent in "Waiting for Sebastian." In "Shotgun Cheatham's Last Night Above Ground," Mrs. Wilcox's ungrammatical cry: "The dead is walking, and Mrs. Dowdel's gunning for me!" Then at the end of the scene Grandma Dowdel's deadpan: "Time you kids was in bed."

In another world entirely, in "Fluffy the Gangbuster," a cat and dog converse across a slight language (and intellectual) barrier. Fluffy hisses, "I'm scared. See me tremble . . . I'm puss shaking in my boots." She's inspired by the cat character in Richard Adams's *Watership Down*. Grover the dog demonstrates his lower intellect by saying "like" too often.

Then there's the title character of "The Most Important Night of Melanie's Life." The extreme difference in how she speaks to her brothers and how she speaks to the all-too-heavenly hunk, Ben, tells us what we need to know about her. "Like make my day, right?"

Writers are collectors of voices, and writing is the art of listening. And we need the vocabulary to give our characters the gift of speech. Learn five new words a day.

And only one more hint. Too many hints might keep you from your own writing:

HINT #5:
A STORY IS A QUESTION ABOUT CHANGE

The story answers the question: How does a character change? This involves plot: the sequence of events, a tight thread in short fiction. It involves a careful blend of word and deed. A story that's all talk is a chat room. A story that's all action is a video game.

At the end of "Priscilla and the Wimps" Monk Klutter is literally in a different place. Word and deed—and Priscilla—have brought him here. This is the simplest story in the collection, pared to essentials, because I was told to make it short.

"Shadows" is probably the most complex of all these stories. It depends upon an elaborate back story about why a girl is being brought up in that old house by two not-quite aunts, and the unspoken motives of those aunts. By means of closely pruned details, we move through her coming-of-age until she learns enough truth to leave.

Movement. Always movement because life itself too often seems to stand still, especially when you're young. At the end of "The Electric Summer," a farm girl who has seen the world's fair wonders how she can just go home now, to things as they were.

"You won't have to, you and the boys," her mother says. "It's your century. It can take you wherever you want to go . . . I'll keep you back if I can. But I'll let you go if I must."

Those are maybe the most loving lines in this collection, in a story that ends at a new beginning, as stories do. Stories end in the dawning hope that there's a lot of life yet to be lived, especially if your characters are young, and your readers are too.

Finally, more than a hint. When we're not writing, we're thinking about writing. And we're writing a lot, in scraps of stolen time other people don't notice they have. After all, we have all these lives we need to be living. And we write and write, to see how the story ends.

"I write," William Faulkner said, "when the spirit moves. And it moves every day."

I conclude with those words from a master of the form because nobody but a reader ever became a writer.